1715

1715

~~~~~~~

JAMES KNEPTON

~~~~~~~

Castaway Publishers

Castaway Publishers
2005 North Meridian Road
Tallahassee, Florida 32303

Library of Congress Cataloging-in-Publication Data has been applied for
1715
James Knepton

ISBN: 978-0-692-39042-9

Cover: Historical 17th Century Map – West Indies
Courtesy of: State Archives of Florida

Printed in the United States of America

To Ariana
Faith Makes Anything Possible,
But Not Easy!

Prologue

Spain's armada fleets plundered an enormous amount of new world wealth from Central and South America during the sixteenth and seventeenth centuries. The period from 1556 to 1710 saw over ten billion dollars in gold, silver, emeralds and pearls transported from Cartagena, Portobello, and Vera Cruz by the Spanish armadas to Spain's port at Seville.

Prior to the development of the armada system in 1556, other countries and pyrates wrecked mayhem on the Spanish treasure ships attempting to get their share of the gold and silver pouring out of the new mines in New Spain (Mexico), Terra Firma (Colombia), and Peru (Potosi mine).

French, English, and Dutch pyrates, some operating under the authority of greedy monarchs to steal and kill at sea and others that were "just plain honest pyrates," were relentless in their pursuit of the valuable cargos being carried by the Spanish vessels.

Growing tired of the constant harassment by pyrates and after the French ransacked and burned Havana in 1555, King Phillip II appointed Pedro Menendez de Aviles as a special maritime advisor to design a system for operating the treasure fleets. Menendez proposed fortified main port of call bases, naval patrols at vulnerable points, and heavily guarded armadas, recommendations that were all implemented during the 1560's.

Henceforth and each year thereafter, the New Spain Armada and the Terra Firma Armada of ships would leave Seville loaded with merchant goods to be traded at Cartagena and Vera Cruz. They worked their way down the coast of Africa and then over to the Windward Islands where they separated.

The New Spain Armada sailed for Vera Cruz where it unloaded its mercury and European cargos and took on millions of silver pesos for the Kings treasury. The Terra Firma Armada sailed for Cartagena and Portobello where they unloaded their merchant cargos and picked up the fortune in gold, silver, emeralds, and pearls to be taken back to Seville. At times, the two armadas would rendezvous in Havana to repair their ships and prepare for the long voyage back together to Spain.

The new armada system established that two fighting galleons must accompany each fleet of ships to protect the armada. The Capitana was the lead galleon carrying the commanding officer and armed with 50 to 70 cannons. The Almiranta galleon brought up the stern and carried the admiral (second in command) with approximately the same number of cannons. Additional warships were added for protection when the silver cargo was extraordinary or during war time.

The added protection proved effective because rarely was a Spanish armada taken down by another attacking force, be it another country or pyrates. However, the one element that all the protection in the world could not defend against was a hurricane.

[1,4]

16th Century Spanish Armada Shipwrecks

One of the earliest known Spanish Armadas to be wrecked by a hurricane was in 1502 when the *De Torres Armada* of thirty-two vessels was annihilated near the Hispaniola coast. The hurricanes wind and waves tore the fleet apart, sinking dozens of ships in the Mona Passage and sending the rest onto the shores of Puerto Rico, Santo Domingo, and the Mona islands. Twenty-seven ships, 500 lives, and a treasure of gold and pearls were lost to the sea in depths of up to one thousand feet. One of the lost artifacts was a solid gold table weighing one a half tons, a gift from Bobadilla to the Catholic Kings for his appointment as governor. [1,3]

The 200 ton nao, the *Visitacion*, was one of the first hurricane wrecked Spanish ships in the Florida Keys when it was dashed to pieces along with its treasure on the reefs. In 1550, *Captain Pedro de la Torre* was sailing the ship from Vera Cruz to Spain when a hurricane drove her onto the *Los Martyrs*, a stretch of reefs from Lower Matecumbe to Elliott Key. [1,2]

Sixteen ships of the *Spanish Armada of Columbus*, laden with 30,000,000 pesos in gold and silver, were wrecked by a hurricane in 1553. The sixteen vessels were preparing to leave the Santo Domingo harbor when the hurricane struck, wrecking thirteen ships in port and driving three ships onto the reefs of Andres Point. The armada of sixteen vessels had assembled at the harbor after loading silver from Vera Cruz, gold from Cartagena, and pearls from the Antilles. [1,3]

Three galleons of the New Spain Armada that left Vera Cruz in 1553 were destroyed by a hurricane soon after leaving the harbor. The galleons were heavily laden with silver from the mines of Mexico and were wrecked near the bars of Isla Blanca. Three hundred Survivors who made it to the beaches were soon surrounded by natives who at first helped them with fire and fish to eat. However, several days later the natives turned on the survivors and slaughtered most of them. Fray Marcos de Mena escaped with several arrows in his body and one arrow in his right eye. Eventually, after help from friendly natives, he made it back to Vera Cruz and was able to tell the story and death of the three hundred shipwrecked survivors. [1,3]

Three treasure ships of the 1554 Terra Firma Armada were wrecked along the coast of Florida by a hurricane near Rio Palmas in 26 degrees and 30 minutes of latitude. The 220 ton *San Esteban (Captain Francisco del Mercerno)* lost all of her gold to the Aix Indians. The 350 ton *Santa Maria del Carmen (Captain Diego Diaz)* and the 200 ton *Santa Maria de Yciar (Captain Alonso Ozosi)* were both salvaged by the Spanish. [1,6]

The Spanish galleon, *Santa Maria La Madalena*, was sailing from Vera Cruz to Spain in 1563, loaded with silver and gold, when she was driven onto a shoal off Cape Canaveral by a hurricane. *Captain Cristobel Rodriquez* was returning to Spain with 50 tons of silver in bullion and coins, 170 boxes of worked silver (candle sticks and plates), and 1,100 pounds of gold when the hurricane hit leaving only 16 out of the 300 passengers and crew to survive the shipwreck. [2,4]

Several galleons of the 1567 Terra Firma Spanish Armada were wrecked on the reefs surrounding Dominica Island by a hurricane. The galleons carried over 3,000,000 pesos in gold, silver, and pearls that were loaded at Cartagena and the Antilles. Carib natives caught and ate most of the survivors and stripped the broken ships of everything they could take. Some of the survivors who were not caught by the natives hid some of the treasure in caves near the beach. [1,3,4]

Two Spanish galleons were wrecked by a hurricane along the Florida coast in 1571. The galleons went down several leagues south of Cape Canaveral drowning all of the passengers and crew save but a few survivors who were able to reach Saint Augustine by longboat. The 300 ton *San Ignacio (Captain Juan de Canovas)* and the 340 ton *Santa Maria de la Limpia Concepcion (captain unknown)* carried over 2,500,000 pesos for which the Spanish salvage ships searched relentlessly but never found. [2,4]

All of the gold, silver, and emeralds taken by the Spanish were at the expense of the Mayan and Inca people who lost their lives to the Spanish invasion and occupation. Peru's native population dropped from 8 million at the time of the conquest to 2 million a century later. Their decedents were forced or paid a pittance to toil relentlessly in the gold, silver, and emerald mines of Central and South America. The mines were often called by the Spaniards "the mouth of hell into which a great mass of people entered every year and never escaped." [3,4]

17th Century Spanish Armada Shipwrecks

General Luis Hernandez de Cordova commanded the Terra Firma Armada of 1605 as it sailed from Cartagena bound for Havana to rendezvous with the New Spain Armada. As Cordova's armada approached the Serranilla Banks to the south of Cuba a hurricane hurled four of the seven galleons onto its reefs where they were "torn to bits on its shallow teeth." They were the 600 ton galleon *San Roque (Captain Ruy Lopez)*, the 750 ton galleon *San Domingo (Captain Diego Ramirez)*, the 500 ton galleon *Nuestra Senora de Begona (Captain Pedro Munoz)*, and the 450 ton galleon *San Ambrosio (Captain Martin de Ormachea)*. The four galleons were carrying an estimated 8,000,000 pesos worth of silver, gold, and emeralds that were lost on the reefs as were the lives of the 1,300 passengers and crew. [1,4]

Four ships from the New Spain Armada and the Terra Firma Armada of 1606 were sunk by a hurricane in the New Channel for Spain. Three of the ships that were attached to *General Luis de Cordoba's* Terra Firma Armada were wrecked and sank off the Florida Keys. The fourth ship, "*Captain Domingo de Licona's Trinidad*, a 350 ton nao of the New Spain Armada under *General Francisco de Corral*, capsized in the howling wind and sank with all her crew and cargo." Hundreds of lives and 1,000,000 pesos in gold and silver went down with the four ships in the deep channel. [1]

The Terra Firma Armada of 1622, commanded by the *Margues de Cadereita*, sailed from Havana and two days later was ripped apart by a hurricane. There were eight registry

6

galleons (600 tons each), seventeen cargo naos (200 tons each) and three patahes (100 tons each) in the armada that was hit by the hurricane on September 6, 1622. Three treasure galleons, the *Santa Margarita*, the *Nuestra Senora Del Rosario*, and the *Nuestra Senora de Atocha*, all heavily laden with gold and emeralds from Colombia, silver from Peru, and pearls from Margarita, were all sent to their graves just west of the Florida Keys. The 600 ton galleon *Santa Margarita (Captain Don Bernardino de Lugo)* was wrecked on one of the keys of the Los Martires. The galleon carried over 500,000 pesos in silver and gold which was lost on the reefs as were most of the passengers and crew. The 600 ton galleon *Nuestra Senora del Rosario (Captain Miguel de Chazarreta)* was wrecked at the Dry Tortugas. The majority of her over 500,000 pesos in silver and gold was recovered and most of her passengers and crew survived. The 600 ton galleon *Nuestra Senora de Atocha (Admiral Pedro Pasquir and Captain Jacome de Veider)* was taken down at Matacumbe Key along with nearly all of her passengers and crew. The *Atocha* had a cargo of over 1,000,000 pesos in silver, gold, emeralds, and pearls and her location was found by a Spanish salvage ship. A buoy was placed to mark the shipwreck location just before another hurricane came through the keys. After the hurricane passed the Spanish could never relocate the Atocha. [1,2,3,4,5]

The Almiranta of *General Antonio de Oquendo's* 1623 New Spain Armada and two treasure galleons, the *Santisima Trinidad* and the *El Aspiritu Santo*, sank 25 miles to the east of the Florida coast after being struck by a hurricane. The 600 ton *Santisima Trinidad (Captain Ysidro de Cepeda)* and the 600 ton *El Aspiritu Santo (Captain Antonio de Sota)* each carried

1,000,000 pesos in silver when they sank to the bottom along with all lives on board. The Almiranta of the armada was able to offload half of her treasure onto smaller ships along with the passengers and crew before sinking with over 1,000,000 pesos in her hull. [1,3]

Fifty ships of the 1626 New Spain and Terra Firma Armada's were hit by a hurricane as they approached Bermuda. The Armada's were escorted by thirteen galleons under *General Larraspuru* and all the ships and galleons were scattered across the ocean by the force of the hurricane winds. The Almiranta of the New Spain Armada had left Vera Cruz with 2,000,000 pesos in silver and she and another merchant vessel went down with all the valuable cargo and 400 out of the 700 crew and passengers. [1]

The *Nuestra Senora De La Concepcion*, the Almiranta of the New Spain Armada carrying 2,000,000 pesos in gold and silver, and five other ships of the armada were wrecked by a hurricane in 1641. The five ships were carrying 1,000,000 pesos in silver and were wrecked along the coast of Florida near Hillsboro Inlet with a great loss of life due to sharks and Indians. The *Concepcion* lost all of her masts and drifted until she wrecked on Abrojos, north of Hispaniola, where the crew piled the gold and silver from the ship's hull onto the reef. Out of the Almiranta's 525 passengers and crew, only 200 remained alive. [1,2,3,4,5]

The Almiranta of the 1656 Terra Firma Armada, carrying over 5,000,000 pesos in gold and silver, was struck by the Capitana of the armada during a hurricane and sank in six fathoms of water "on the shoals of Los Mimbras." The *Nuestra Senora De los Maravillas* had picked up her gold and silver at Cartagena and was under the command of *Captain Matias de Orellana*. The Capitana *(Jesus Maria under the command of Captain Juan de Hoyos)* plowed into the *Las Maravillas* during the storm as they were entering the Bahama Channel. The *Las Maravillas* quickly filled with water and sank, carrying 605 crew and passengers to their deaths along with the fortune in gold and silver. [1,3,4,5]

A 700 ton galleon in the Terra Firma Armada of 1683 with 1,800,000 pesos in registered gold and silver was sunk near the Florida coast during a hurricane. The galleon was also carrying 77 chests of pearls, 49 chests of emeralds, 217 chests of orient goods, and passenger chests which probably held another fortune in unregistered gold and silver. The *Santissima Concepcion commanded by Admiral Manual Ortiz Arosemena* was totally destroyed after striking a shallow during the storm. Only 4 out of the 500 crew and passengers reached the coast and made it to Saint Augustine. [1,3]

These shipwrecks represent only a sample of the over 70 Spanish Armada treasure wrecks caused by hurricanes that occurred during the 16th and 17th centuries. Just a prelude to one of the most devastating shipwreck disasters in the history of Spain's treasure fleets.

16th and 17th Century Related Terms

Armada
System developed in the 1560's where war galleons (Capitana and Almiranta) were added to protect the New Spain fleet and the Terra Firma fleet sailing from Seville, Spain to the new world and returning to Spain with the plunder from Central and South America.

Almiranta
The rear war galleon of the armada that carried the admiral and the King's treasure. The admiral was second in authority and took command when there was fighting or the General could no longer convey orders.

Capitana
The lead war galleon that accompanied the armada, carrying the Kings treasure and the commanding officer or general who was responsible for the guns, charts, soldiers, adequate provisions, and safety of the fleets.

Cartagena
Founded in 1533, the city had a population of two thousand prosperous Spaniards and was defended by massive forts. Cartagena was the anchorage of the Terra Firma Armada, the headquarters of the New Granada Viceroyalty, and by 1650 it was the most important city in all of the West Indies.

Frigate
In action with all European fleets by 1640, this class of ship was fast and maneuverable, ballasted between 900 to 1700 tons, and carried anywhere from 36 to 72 cannons.

Galleon
Ships of this class were used for fighting and convoy. They were heavily armed, only

carrying the King's registered treasure, varying from 700 to 2000 tons, and carrying up to 90 cannons.

Hispaniola — Rendezvous point for the first fleets of Spanish ships in the 1500's, carrying plundered gold, silver and emeralds from Central and South America back to Spain. Eventually Havana took its place as the main staging area for the armadas and Hispaniola became a haven for English, French and Dutch, pyrates.

New Spain Armada — Fleet of ships that sailed once a year from Spain to New Spain (Vera Cruz), carrying mercury for silver mining and returning to Spain with the wealth extracted from Central America.

Peso — At this time, a peso was worth one troy ounce of silver.

Portobello — After reaching Cartagena, the Capitana and Almiranta of the Terra Firma Armada would sail to Portobello to load on the silver from the mines in Peru.

Privateer — During war, Kings and government would contract with the captains and crew of sailing ships to destroy and kill their adversary on the high seas. Spain was a favorite target because of the great wealth being transferred from the new world back to Seville.

Pyrate — The word pyrate is the old English spelling used in Captain Charles Johnson's 1724 publication, *A General History of the Pyrates*. Many pyrates originated as privateer's who would not stop their once government sanctioned enterprise. Most captured pyrates ended up swinging from the gallows and some were then hung in cages at a harbor entrance to warn of the risk of unsanctioned pyracy.

Terra Firma Armada   A fleet of ships that sailed once a year from Spain to Terra Firma (Colombia). The merchant ships offloaded and traded their European goods for the new world wealth at Cartagena. The King's galleons would sail to Portobello to pick up the silver from Peru then return to Cartagena to escort the armada back to Spain.

Vera Cruz   At the time, a hole in the wall like Portobello, it only came alive when the New Spain Armada arrived to trade goods and to offload the mercury for the mines in New Spain (Mexico). Then, trading goods from Manila and the silver from the New Spain mines was loaded onto the ships for the return trip to Spain.

[1,4,10,11,14]

£

Part I

Terra Firma

Chapter 1

The end of the War of Spanish Succession in 1714 saw establishments filled with jubilant sailors by the hundreds celebrating and making their way back to home and families. The war's ending, after thirteen years of bitter sea battles, reunited English seamen and their families after years of separation and hardship at home and away.

Sailors sometimes had experienced extreme cruelty under England's oppressive naval war machine but it became even tougher as seaman jobs dwindled under peace time's austerity. Many of the ships that had survived monumental naval engagements and brutal fighting ended up being idled at port. The need to acquire a ship's crew was rapidly diminishing as the war ships disappeared from the oceans and the sailors soon realized that they had to fight a new and different economic battle. [1,11]

Unable to find work many seamen in desperation turned their eyes towards the Spanish Main and the gold and silver that the Spanish Galleons were bringing back from Cartagena, Portobello, Vera Cruz, and Manila. Tales of extraordinary riches being brought across the ocean from the Spanish Main were evidenced by wrecked Spanish Armada fleets that were torn apart by hurricanes and their treasure laid bare for the taking along the primitive coasts of Florida.

The Spanish Main in 1714 was bustling with commerce and the over 2,500 Spanish families who had settled there were growing prosperous on the mining of Terra Firma's gold and emeralds and the trading of their accumulated wealth with Spain. The commercial impact of Cartagena on the development of the new world had grown as intensely as the vast amount of treasure being plundered and sent back to Spain.

After years of Spanish military control, many private families emerged as the owners of the gold and emerald mines throughout the mountainous region of Terra Firma. The Vasquez family was one of the first to establish a presence in the mining of its gold and grew wealthy at the expense of the natives who toiled deep in the mines for only a few pesos each month.

The children of the Vasquez family, Juan, Maria, and Carmen, grew up helping their father to control their gold mines and manage their large estate between the mountains and the heavily fortified city of Cartagena. It was dangerous work with mines being shut down due to rock slides or the natives rebelling because of the often gruel treatment received from overbearing foremen.

The children vaguely remembered their mother for she had died in an accident when they were very young, leaving their father to care for them and the family business. Their father was a generous man and a shrewd businessman who had prospered along with the other families of Cartagena.

The family traveled at least once a month to their gold mines, checking on the mines operations and consulting with the foremen about the workers and production quotas. Natives from nearby villages worked in very dangerous conditions to extract the gold that was made into jewelry, gold chains, or gold bars and then placed in chests for the journey to Spain.

The children would usually make the trip all together with their father, but this time was different. Alonso had received word that a landslide had occurred at the El Grado mine and that several of the workers and natives had been injured.

"Carmen, let's go girl, the day grows shorter and the horses are becoming impatient," Alonso shouted standing at the bottom of the stairs.

"Coming father, I could not find my other boot," Carmen shouted back.

"You are just like your mother, beautiful but very slow," Alonso declared as she was coming down the stairs.

Juan, Alonso's only son, had grabbed something to eat from the kitchen and met his father in the hall way on his way out.

"Juan I need you to take Emilio, Antonio and several wagons to pick up the supplies in Cartagena. Here is a list of what we will need to get the mine back in operation," Alonso said as he handed the list to Juan.

"Get what you can and make haste in joining us, but be careful on the mountain roads my son," Alonso shouted out the warning to Juan as he rushed out the front door.

"Okay my lovely senoritas, do you have enough of everything for three weeks?" Alonso asked his two daughters as they stepped out the front door.

"Yes father, do not worry about us. Did you bring everything you will need?" Carmen asked as the girls untied the reins to their horses.

"Yes senorita, I have everything," Alonso replied laughingly as he threw their bags to Miguel who was waiting in the wagon. Then they all mounted their horses and started off toward the mountains.

It was a three day ride to reach the mine so when they reached the La Magdalena River just before sundown, they camped close to the river's edge. The river was higher than usual due to heavy rainfall in the mountains, which is what Alonso suspected was the cause of the catastrophe at the mine. Alonso and Miguel set up the tents and got a fire going just in time for the girls to come running into camp with several large trout.

"See father, your daughters can catch fish with the best and we cleaned them too," Carmen boasted as she handed the fish to her father.

"It just goes to prove that I taught my daughters well," Alonso replied jokingly and proudly took the fish to be roasted on the fire.

Sitting around the campfire, Alonso remembered the times when he and his wife Isabella would camp and ride for days in this valley.

"Just below the mountains, the rolling foot hills were covered with large trees, carpets of green grass, and you could see flocks of parrots that would glide across the hills for as far as the eye could see," Alonso sighed with a hint of grief. "I miss your mother very much," Alonso added.

"Father, did mother like to fish as much as we do?" Carmen asked.

"Yes, she caught more fish than all of us put together and she knew how to cook them on the open fire better than all of us, too!" Alonso said laughing and remembering how Isabella brought joy into everything she touched.

"Yes, Isabella loved everything about this valley, she loved all of her children, and she loved life," Alonso proclaimed as he handed his daughters some of the roasted fish.

"When I look at both of my daughters I see the spirit and energy that your mother had for life. She kept me on the right path and out of trouble many times as she did for the both of you," Alonso admitted as he built the fire up for the night.

"Why have you never spoken to us about our mother's passing?" Carmen asked her father.

"I guess my princess, because up till now it has been too painful to speak about what happened on that miserable night," Alonso said as he hesitated and stoked the fire as the sparks flew into the night air.

"We had just finished inspecting the Escondido gold mine and were making our way up the mountain to the El Grado mine. A storm moved in quickly with heavy rains and lightning and the rain water came rushing down the sides of the mountain," Alonso said as he gestured with his hand in a downward movement.

"I yelled to Miguel and your mother to unhook the horses from the wagon but it was too late as part of the mountain gave way onto the road and the horses reared up in fright," Alonso said with his voice starting to quiver.

"Miguel tried to calm the horses but when lightning struck again, the horses bolted upwards throwing your mother out of the wagon and over the side of the mountain," Alonso said as the wind blew smoke in his face and his eyes began to water.

"We went back down the mountain, searching behind every boulder and in every crevice until we reached the valley below," Alonso said with sorrow in his heart.

"I searched but could never find your mother's body. My children, she loved you with all her soul and you must always keep her close to your heart as well," Alonso said as he put more wood on the fire.

"Now my children, off to bed and get a good night's sleep, we have a long ride to Los Royes tomorrow," Alonso told the girls as they ran off to their tent.

Alonso and Miguel kept the fire blazing, swapping tales long into the night and remembering the adventures of carving out a new existence in an unforgiving land.

There were many obstacles that they had overcome in developing and growing their business in the new world. Facing down death itself was the most challenging, in an often treacherous and sometimes fatal business.

Chapter 2

Los Royes was a frontier town started in the conquistador days when the Spanish invaders sought gold in the mountains of Terra Firma. The town developed over the years as a gold exchange and stepping off base into the mountains where the first gold mines originated. It was always a rough place where foremen, miners and merchants carried out any type of transaction that involved the gold that was extracted from the mines penetrating deep inside the mountains.

In the early days, the Spanish Military controlled the town and maintained law and order among the civilians. As the easy gold dwindled, the military relaxed their control and opportunistic citizens moved in to operate the mines. Mario Cardina was a friendly rival of Alonso and over the years they had both competed for the purchase of gold mines that the military no longer wanted to operate.

"Carmen and Maria, let's camp here along the river," Alonso said as they watered their horses at a river close to Los Royes.

"I am going into Los Royes to check on business and to see how Mario is doing," Alonso told the girls.

"Father please be careful, remember what happened last time," Carmen replied.

"I haven't forgotten. Catch us some trout that you can be proud of and I will return just in time for dinner," Alonso jokingly told the girls before he turned his horse and started towards the bridge that led to town.

Miguel and the girls would be busy setting up camp and preparing to fish, so Alonso was not uncomfortable about leaving the girls at the campsite. Above all, he wanted to keep the girls exposure to the vices found in the little town at the foot of the mountains to a minimum.

Alonso crossed the bridge and headed into town, remembering what Carmen had said at the river. It was unfortunate that Carmen had witnessed a killing in the town when Mario and another speculator had a bitter argument over the purchase of an extremely lucrative gold mine.

The speculator accused Mario of bribing the officials, which he probably did, and attacked Mario in broad daylight. Mario was able to turn the pistol back towards the speculator and he died where he fell. Mario was an opportunist who had a family and not a ruthless murderer as some had led others to believe.

Arriving in Los Royes, Alonso first went to the local tavern to learn if any messages had been left for him. One message was urgent saying that Mario wanted to see him as soon as he arrived. Alonso had a drink and spoke to several of the other owners before traveling to Mario's hacienda.

Mario was in good spirits and it appeared that the previous incident had quieted down. However, Alonso could tell that he had some serious business to discuss as they entered his office in the back of his home.

"Alonso, I'm selling everything and going back to Spain. My family comes first and it's time to return to Seville while we are all still alive," Mario said solemnly as he offered Alonso a pipe to smoke.

"Mario, it's going to be a huge change for you and your family. Will you be able to take care of all your business in time to sail with the armada at Cartagena?" Alonso asked as he packed the pipe with his own tobacco.

"Yes, we started the preparations just after the incident occurred. My wife said no more and it would be better for all of us to return to Spain," Mario said assuredly.

"Alonso, we still have one matter that is unresolved. As you know, I have had partners for most of the gold mines that I own and they have bought out my interest in all of them. The last gold mine that I purchased is still for sale and I wanted to offer it to you first, because of our friendship," Mario proposed as he lit his pipe.

"Mario, this is all a shock that you will be leaving. You are my best competition. Who will I spar with after you leave?" Alonso laughingly responded as Mario joined in the laughter between two old competitors, but friends none the less.

"Of course I will purchase the mine, and thank you old friend for thinking about me," Alonso said as they both stood up and shook hands on the agreement. Alonso was excited about the purchase because he knew, when the Spanish military had decided to abandon the gold mine, others were speculating there was a substantial amount of gold left to be extracted.

Alonso returned to the campsite in high spirits and just in time as Carmen and Maria had finished cooking the fish and had begun sampling it as Alonso rode his horse into camp.

While they all ate, Alonso shared the news about purchasing the new mine and Mario's decision to return to Spain. The girls immediately started asking their father about his life in

Spain and the three of them, along with Miguel, spent hours talking and laughing about it late into the night.

They were off early the next morning, heading up the mountain side on a narrow path built by the natives. A wagon drawn by horses could just barely make it at the tightest of places. By noon they were half way to the mine and the path was starting to narrow at the curves. Along the way the girls noticed the caves dug out by the natives that were used as resting places from the backbreaking work it took to forge out the road that spiraled around the mountain.

"Patron, the wagon," Miguel yelled out to Alonso.

They turned to see Miguel jumping from the wagon and then unhitching the horses from the teetering wagon. The back wheel was hanging over the cliff and the wagon was leaning heavily towards flipping over altogether.

Alonso rushed back to the wagon, tied a rope to the rear axle, and hitched the horses to the rope. By pulling just enough to bring the rear wheel back onto the rocks the wagon was once again safe to travel.

As evening approached they finally reached the mine and were greeted by the foreman, Diego. Loyal and trusted, Diego had worked for Alonso ever since the mine had been purchased eighteen years ago when Carmen was born.

Diego could not stop talking in order to let Alonso know of everything, how the landslide had blocked the mines entrance, how many of the natives had died and how many were still in the mine. The natives had made good progress in clearing the boulders away from the entrance and were ready to move the remaining rocks.

"Caution Patron, we are still having tremors and the mountain could come down on us again," Diego warned pointing to a cliff jutting out near the top of the mountain.

"Carmen and Maria I want you to stay back, it's still too dangerous," Alonso shouted to the girls.

Just as he was warning the girls, the earth began to shake, the mountain cracked, and a wall of rocks cascaded down on Alonso, Diego, and the rest of the natives.

In a matter of seconds the girls had witnessed the loss of their father, their provider, and their protector. The scene was horrific and the anguished cries from the few who were still alive was too terrible to imagine.

The girls were stunned and could not move. Maria started crying and Carmen consoled her until she was able to calm down. Carmen loved her father deeply but she was stronger and more resilient than Maria.

"Miguel you have to go to the village to get help," Carmen shouted as she and Maria started moving the injured natives away from the rock slide.

The native villagers arrived and they worked through the night digging out the bodies of Alonso, Diego and the members of their tribe. The opening to the mine was now completely covered with large boulders. The natives who were trapped in the first collapse were now presumed dead and prayers were given for their departure.

By morning all the bodies had been recovered from around the mine entrance and the natives departed taking their dead tribe members back to their village for burial. The natives would not want to enter this mine again and they would recall it only as a place of death.

The bodies of Alonzo and Diego were disfigured from the rock slide and needed burial immediately. Miguel dug two graves close to the mine while the girls cut up parts of their tent to make two burial sleeves.

Prayers were offered, Alonso and Diego were laid to rest, and crosses were placed. It was difficult for the girls in their mourning but they found solace in this tragedy that their father was now in a better place with their mother.

Juan, Emilio, and Antonio arrived in the afternoon and were in disbelief at the deaths of Alonso and Diego. The girls told them about the earthquake and the rocks sliding down on their father, Diego and the natives.

Juan took it very hard, first his mother and now his father by the same mountain. Juan stayed at his father's grave late into the evening when he was joined by Carmen and Maria.

"Our father was a brave man, a kind man, he was good to us all, I will miss him most of all," Carmen said.

"We will all miss him, but now we must be as brave as he was. Our father would want us to carry on as he has told us many times," Juan said as they returned to the camp and then gathered around the fire.

"I never told you this because I never dreamed that anything would happen to our father. He told me that if anything should happen to him that we should take our wealth and return to Spain to be close to our mothers parents," Juan said as he added more wood to the fire..

"This is a dangerous business and our father had the military backing to carry out the transactions and to keep everyone in their place. Eventually, he wanted us all to leave Cartagena and sail to Spain for a better life," Juan told the girls.

"But Juan all of our friends and family are here, how can we just up and leave them all behind?" Maria asked apprehensively.

"They are all thinking the same," Juan replied.

"Remember six years ago when the English attacked and devastated the last armada just outside the harbor of Cartagena?" Juan asked the girls.

"Maria, you were very young and might not remember that our parents and grandparents were terribly upset. Our cousin Armando was on the *San Martin*, which only by the grace of God was able to escape and return to the safety of the harbor," Carmen said as she shifted the logs on the fire.

"It was a great loss for many families, the *San Jose* was destroyed along with over 500 passengers and crew, the *Gobierno* was captured, and the *urca* was set afire so the English could not capture her," Juan told Maria as he placed another log on the fire.

"And what about our mother's two sisters who left for Spain three years ago and have written that they now do not plan to return. The time to leave is now," Juan said stepping back from the fire as the flames grew taller.

"Juan, how would we do this, what about the other mines and our hacienda? Would we sell them?" Carmen asked anxiously.

"We will work with our Uncle Eduardo to get all of our affairs in order and discuss with him what to do about the ranch. Since our grandmother is living with us he might decide to take it over and run it himself," Juan explained, trying to convince the girls to do what their father had advised.

"For now I will take Emilio, Antonio, and the three wagons to collect the gold in our mines and make final

29

settlements with the workers and natives. The foremen over the mines can return with us to guard the gold on our trip home and I will pay them well to do so," Juan said solemnly as they all stared at the flames of the fire.

"I think your right, maybe it is time to go to Spain where we could live near our grandparents and relatives," Carmen said looking at Maria.

"Yes, in that case I see no reason to stay. Maybe grandmother will go with us as well," Maria said hopefully.

"Okay sisters, then we have a plan, let's try and get some sleep and have an early start in the morning," Juan said as they all stood up and embraced one another.

There was little sleep as they all kept thinking about their parents and leaving home. It was now a new day and they all realized that they were truly on their own, to make their own decisions, right or wrong. So, before light and without breakfast, Juan, Emilio and Antonio set out for the other mines and Carmen, Maria, and Miguel headed back to the ranch to tell their grandmother about their father and her son.

Chapter 3

General Antonio de Echeverz was the commander of the Terra Firma Armada of four ships that had arrived from Spain in August, 1714. General Echeverz's fleet was comprised of privately owned vessels that were given contracts by the King to pick up the spoils from Terra Firma and Portobello and return them to Spain. In addition to the gold, silver, and emeralds other valuable cargo would be loaded onboard including cocoa, brazil wood, hides, and tobacco. All were in great demand throughout Europe and would command a high price. The General's Capitana was the *Nuestra Senora de la Carmen*, the fifty-two cannon flagship of the fleet captained by Armando Sanchez. [7]

"Captain Sanchez, Eduardo Vasquez is on the main deck and has requested to meet with you," the quartermaster said.

"Tell him I'll be there in one minute," Armando replied as he finished signing the ship's log, stored away his papers, and then made his way to the main deck.

"Eduardo, my favorite cousin, it's great to see you, how have you been?" Armando asked.

"Quite well cousin and what about your new wife?" Eduardo asked.

"She's doing well from what I hear, I never get to see her doing the King's work," Armando jokingly replied.

"So, are you ready to make another shipment?" Armando asked.

"In a way, yes, but differently," Eduardo replied.

Alonso and Eduardo were partners in mining the gold and would give Armando a commission so that he would see that the gold made it to their business investors in Spain. Armando was happy to do it and the brother's paid their cousin a significant remuneration to make sure that the gold arrived safely in Seville.

"Armando, Alonso was killed in a rockslide and I am thinking about getting out of that business. It is dangerous work and not worth dying for anymore," Eduardo said.

"Saints above, first Isabella and now Alonso, Eduardo I am so sorry, what can I do to help?" Armando asked.

"Alonso's children would like to go to Spain and live with Isabella's parents until they can find a place of their own. I know all the passenger positions must have been taken months ago but is there any way that you can find passage for them?" Eduardo asked.

"There is a family who may have to stay here because the wife is ill and if it's true then she may not be able to travel. We are sailing in a few days to Portobello and will return in several months, I will try to have word to you about the passage before we leave," Armando promised.

"When you return we expect you to come out to the hacienda and stay with us for as long as you want, you can get your land legs back and help us with the cattle," Eduardo laughed as he extended his hand.

"I will gladly visit and help with the cattle to get a steak dinner," Armando replied laughing as he shook Eduardo's hand.

The Capitana was a large war galleon that was responsible for carrying the King's share of the treasure and protected the other merchant ships in the fleet from privateers and pyrates. Before leaving for Portobello to pick up the King's silver from Peru, Armando sent word to Eduardo that there was a cabin for Juan, Maria and Carmen. A few weeks later the children and their grandmother went to see Eduardo and his family.

"Children, great news, Armando got you a cabin on the General's Capitana and the fleet will sail in the spring," Eduardo told them as he met them at the front door.

"That's excellent news, thank you uncle, we know it was you who persuaded Armando," Juan said.

"You know Armando, as a member of the family he can always be counted on when we need him," Eduardo explained.

"Uncle Eduardo, can we talk privately?" Juan asked.

"Of course Juan, let's go to my study," Eduardo said leading the way.

"Uncle Eduardo, I wanted to make sure you were okay with what I did with the mines?" Juan asked.

"Yes Juan, under the circumstances you did exactly what I would have done. There has been too much blood for the mines to continue, first your mother and now your father. I am not going to reopen the mines until we can think more clearly about what to do next," Eduardo explained.

"We melted the gold and I paid the foremen their commissions. They wanted to know what was next and I told them that you and I would discuss our position and let them know as soon as we decided," Juan said.

"Good, well done," Eduardo replied.

"I divided the gold into two equal shares and locked it in our safe. It's there for you to pick which share you want," Juan said.

"Thank you Juan, you have done an excellent job. I think we would have been good partners if you had stayed," Eduardo said as he reached for his pipe.

"What do you think we should do about the hacienda?" Juan asked.

"You have a lot of cattle. Why don't you let some of the mine foremen help run the ranch until you get settled in Seville and I can manage it until you decide what to do," Eduardo said lighting his pipe.

"I like the idea, thanks uncle. Did Armando say how many chests we could bring?" Juan asked.

"It's usually two large chests for each person but it can be stretched to three each for the right price," Eduardo said light heartedly as they walked to join the others.

After the fleet returned from Portobello, Armando journeyed to Eduardo's hacienda to see the family. Eduardo proudly showed Armando the improvements they had made to the house and the new garden that his wife Cristina had added near the veranda.

During the next few weeks Eduardo, Armando, and the children would often spend days riding throughout his ranch, herding the cattle over the rolling hills set against the towering mountains of Terra Firma. Eduardo had invested a good portion of his new found wealth into the hacienda where he had established several large herds of cattle that roamed the valley.

One night after dinner, Armando had joined Eduardo in his study.

"Armando, how did it go at Portobello?" Eduardo curiously enquired.

"It all depends on who you believe," Armando replied

"That means you didn't get it?" Eduardo asked.

"The Governor of Peru did not respond to our call for the king's silver. At least that is what General Echeverz told us," Armando said sarcastically.

"That is strange," Eduardo replied.

"My guess is that we went through all the motions of picking up the treasure so that the English would think that we had loaded it on our ships," Armando said.

"I see, it's probably because of the *Nuestra Senora San Jose* sinking to her grave six years ago with tons of rich silver and six hundred Spaniards," Eduardo speculated, grabbing his pipe and offering one to Armando.

"Yes, it was a huge loss for the King to lose the *San Jose* to the English guns. I imagine King Philip ordered General Echeverz to request the transfer by sending the King's letter that had orders to the contrary," Armando replied as he accepted the pipe.

"So what do you think the King ordered?" Eduardo asked as he struck a match to light his pipe.

"I think the King's letter instructed the governor to send the King's silver to Argentina for transport to Spain instead of to Portobello. The King didn't want to lose the silver from Peru to the English again," Armando conjectured as he packed his pipe with tobacco.

"However, this way the English probably think that you are fully loaded with silver," Eduardo worriedly reasoned.

"Yes, but this time we will send out fast sloops in all directions to check for war ships before leaving the harbor. We do not want to end up at the ocean bottom like the *San Jose*," Armando added with a grin as he struck a match and lit up his pipe.

Spanish Galleon *San Jose*

Perhaps one of the richest armadas to ever set sail for Spain was the Terra Firma Armada of 17 ships that left Cartagena on June 8, 1708. The 22,000,000 pesos in silver received at Portobello from Peru was placed on the four armed ships of the fleet: the *Capitana San Jose*, 7,000,000 pesos; the *Almiranta San Martin*, 6,000,000 pesos; the galleon *Gobierno*, 5,000,000 pesos; and the *urca*, 4,000,000 pesos.

Returning to Cartagena the ships took on gold and emeralds from the mountains of Terra Firma for a combined total of at least 34,000,000 pesos in gold, silver, and emeralds distributed among the vessels of the fleet.

No sooner had the fleet left the port of Cartagena when English sails were spotted and the fleet turned and sailed back for the safety of the harbor. The Admiral of the armada ordered the *San Jose*, the *San Martin*, the *Gobierno* and the *urca* to drop back and shield the merchant ships.

English Admiral Commodore Wager engaged the Spanish galleons with the 70 gun *Expedition*, the 60 gun *Kingston*, the 50 gun *Portland* and the fire ship *Vulture*. As the battle raged into the night the *San Jose* blew up and sank in about a thousand feet of water near Baru Island with only 5 of her 600 passengers and crew surviving.

The *Gobierno* was captured, the *San Martin* escaped back to the harbor, and the *urca* was beached and set afire by the Spaniards to prevent English acquisition.

Two English captains were subsequently court martialed for failing to enter the Bay of Cartagena and capture the *San Martin* with her treasure of 6,000,000 pesos in silver. The *San*

Jose lies today just off the coast of Colombia in a thousand feet of water with her 7,000,000 pesos in silver still safely inside her hull. [1,2,3,4]

£

The next morning Eduardo and Armando rode to the hacienda of Juan, Maria and Carmen to discuss the trip.

"Uncle and cousin, it's so good to see you, come in," Juan said as he welcomed Eduardo and Armando into their home. "Come out onto the veranda and I'll get the senoritas."

"Uncle Eduardo and Armando," the girls screamed as they ran onto the veranda and greeted their uncles with hugs and admiration.

They talked for hours about Alonso, Isabella, Armando and everyone else. There was sorrow over Alonso and Isabella and joy over Armando's new wife and perhaps a new baby. After dinner, Juan and Eduardo told Armando they wanted to show him something in their vault.

Near the back of the house, down a flight of steep stairs and through a maze of hallways they finally came to a wooden wall. With the flip of a lever the door opened to the glow of shimmering gold and there on the floor were two large piles of gold bars.

"One share belongs to the children and the other belongs to me," Eduardo said. "The children's share will help them start a new life in Seville and because this is our last investment with the mines, I will split my share three ways: one for my family, one for our mother, and one for Armando's new family."

Armando could not stop thanking Eduardo for his generosity. "Cousin, what can I ever do to repay you for this glorious gift?" Armando asked.

"Make it three chests for each of the children to take on the voyage and make sure that they arrive safely in Seville," Eduardo joyfully requested.

"Cousin, consider it done," Armando promised.

Chapter 4

"How in the world are we going to get everything into nine chests," Maria proclaimed.

"We are lucky that it is nine instead of six," Juan replied. "I will only need one and we will put the gold and valuables into my other two chests leaving both of you with three each for all of your clothes and shoes," Juan said jokingly.

"Juan, this is no joking matter, we must have everything just right for when we meet our grandparents in Seville," Carmen responded back in a scolding manner.

"Children, you must stop this squabbling and get packed quickly, You have been trying to decide what to take for two days but now it's time to finish packing. Your chests must be at the loading dock by noon tomorrow," Grandmother Teresa said.

"Grandmother, we all wish that you were going with us," Maria said starting to cry and putting her arms around her.

"I know child, but these old bones could not take such a voyage. I will be here waiting for you when you can return," Grandmother Teresa replied giving her granddaughter a hug and a kiss.

The next morning, at the docks of Cartagena, it was chaos as passengers were arriving to board the Capitana and the ship's crew was busy making final preparations for the long voyage. Ranch workers Miguel and Antonio had brought the nine chests to the dock and were making sure that seven of the chests went into the ship's hull and the two marked chests loaded with the children's valuables were placed in their cabin. All the other passengers were doing the same, making sure their chests were loaded on board and their valuables were in a safe place.

The ship was alive with activity, full of nobles and passengers with their families returning to Spain along with all their belongings and the wealth that they had accumulated while in the new world. Even without the King's silver from Peru, the passenger's treasure of gold, silver and emeralds aboard the seven ships of the fleet was immense.

Armando had arranged for the children to share a cabin with Father Francisco who took the children under his wing and showed them around the ship. The ship's deck looked like a tropical jungle with stalks of bananas, fresh mangos, and sacks of oranges brought on board for the voyage. Food and drink provisions had been placed below along with pigs, goats and chickens, whose noises and smells had to be endured by the passengers on the lower decks.

The ship had the daily obligation to provide each passenger with a large biscuit and two pints of drinking water. Grandmother Teresa knew about the rations and supplied the children with wine and dried beef that could be stored in their cabin during the two month voyage.

"Cousin, we are ready to sail, the fast sloops were sent out two days ago and they reported back no sightings of warships," Armando said having to shout above the ship's passenger noise.

"That's good news cousin, have a safe voyage and here is a letter to your new wife from Cristina. We hope to meet her as soon as we can," Eduardo replied shaking Armando's hand.

"Juan, Maria, and Carmen we will miss you and here is a letter for your mother's parents from Cristina and I. They will help you get your new start in Seville," Eduardo said as he hugged each one goodbye.

"My children, God Bless You and God speed you on this voyage," Cristina said as she hugged and kissed each one.

"Goodbye grandmother, I will write often, I love you and will miss you," Maria said as she hugged and kissed Grandmother Teresa.

General Echeverz gave the order to sail and all those going ashore disembarked to the cobblestone streets below filled with excited and jubilant crowds. Father Francisco offered a prayer and Armando had the flag raised to signal the order. A cannon was fired to signal the more distant ships in the fleet and officers shouted orders to deck crews to drop their main sails.

As the *Nuestra Senora de la Carmen* slowly moved forward, Juan, Carmen, and Maria waved farewell intently to their relatives and friends below.

The fleet was sailing for Havana to rendezvous with the New Spain Armada sailing from Vera Cruz and the passage to Havana would take the fleet dangerously close to Jamaica and the Cayman Islands.

Pyrates were known to lay in wait there to ambush the stragglers, taking what they could from the merchant ships before the Capitana and Almiranta would turn about to beat them down.

Aboard the Capitana, the children took turns during the day safeguarding their chests and in their free time they would join the others in card games or simple gossiping.

To break the routine of life aboard the ship, passengers created mock bullfights and celebrated as many religious holidays as possible. Predicting the weather was a continuous source of interest to both sailors and passengers. The cramped quarters, tropical heat, and sometimes bad weather often caused seasickness throughout the ship.

Mario Cardina and his family were passengers on the Capitana, carrying with them all the wealth that they had created from the gold mines of Terra Firma. Mario had been able to settle all of his affairs in Los Royes and was also able to sell the gold mine that Alonso had intended to purchase. Mario and his children thought that they should have at least one mock bullfight before they reached Havana.

The plan was to have everyone pretend that they were in Spain attending a real bullfight along with all the pomp and ceremony. Carmen and all the children sold tickets to the willing passengers for three bull fights the next day and promised an exciting finale.

However unbeknownst to the armada, to the starboard side of the fleet, was a sloop tracking their movements as they sailed closer to the Cayman Islands.

"Steady as she goes Mr. Langford and stay close to the wind!" Captain Charles Vane ordered.

"Aye, Captain!" Mr. Langford replied.

"Tis a beautiful night and tis a grand sight to behold," Captain Vane pondered as he watched the fleet's night lights pitch back and forth in the distance.

"It's in our favor to have only a sliver of a moon and an easterly wind to sail. It will put us directly on this outlier that seems to be moving slowly," Captain Vane declared as he scoped the merchant ship that they had moved upon in the early morning hours.

"Captain, maybe she's taking on water," Mr. Langford suggested as he turned the rudder to fill the main sail.

"Could be Mr. Langford, she's riding mighty low at the water line," Captain Vane replied.

"Mr. Langford we'll take this ship at dawn. We will have to time it precisely at first light to come up on its starboard side, keeping the merchant between us and the Capitana. Can you do it man?" Captain Vane inquired.

"Aye Captain, consider it done!" Mr. Langford boldly declared.

The fleet had managed to stay together during the night with the exception of a few outliers and they were now approaching the Cayman Islands. On the deck of the Capitana the children were calling everyone to come for breakfast before the start of the first bullfight. Carman had picked one of the young girls to take the passengers tickets and to start the event.

Just as soon as some of the passengers had started to arrive on deck, a loud cannon shot rang out in the distance. Everyone rushed to the rail in time to see a merchant ship take a hit on the bow. The merchant ship had strayed too far from the fleet and was now under attack by pyrates sailing a sloop under their black flag. Everyone watched as the pyrate sloop drew closer to the merchant ship and then saw the merchant's sails being raised.

"Mr. Langford, give me the signal when the Capitana turns and makes for us!" Captain Vane ordered.

"Let's go men!" Captain Vane shouted for his men to board the merchant with pistols drawn and knives flashing.

So early in the morning, most of the crew and passengers of the merchant ship were still below decks including the captain. The first mate and the crew on deck had raised their main sail and did not resist the pyrate's orders.

The pyrates took control of the ship and began entering the passenger cabins to relieve them of their valuables. Working quickly the pyrates took the passengers chests and placed them on the main deck.

"Antonio, what are these men doing with the passengers chests?" the merchant captain asked his first mate as he clambered up onto the ship's deck.

"Be silent Captain, abide by our orders and no harm will come to passengers or crew. If not, you'll be the first to swim with the sharks!" Captain Vane assured the merchant Captain.

The pyrates were quick to start transferring the passenger chests to their sloop before the Capitana turned. The pyrates had transferred about fifteen chests when Mr. Langford yelled out that the Capitana was turning.

All eyes quickly looked in the Capitana's direction as it was making its turn toward them.

"Men, that's the last one, back to the ship quickly!" Captain Vane shouted.

"Thank you Captain for not being stupid," Captain Vane said as he jumped over the railing and landed back on his sloop.

"Let go the hooks and cast off!" Captain Vane commanded.

"Now, Mr. Langford, I'll be asking the same. You need to keep the merchant between us and the Capitana as we head southeast," Captain Vane ordered while watching as the Capitana's sails filled with the wind and she started to catch her stride.

The Capitana maneuvered around the merchant ship as quickly as possible to get a clear shot at the pyrate sloop and once she was cleared, she fired all of her starboard cannons.

Only one shot clipped the stern of the sloop, doing little damage. The pyrate sloop was a fast ship and it quickly slipped out of range of the galleon's cannons.

The Capitana turned and drew close to the merchant ship. Officers from the Capitana took a launch and boarded the merchant to check on the passengers and crew. They found that no one was injured, however the pyrates had made off with sixteen chests belonging to the passengers.

It was a devastating loss for those passengers who had their chests stolen by the pyrates. Going back to Spain empty handed was not an option, most of them would get off at Havana and return to Cartegena to try and regain their lost wealth. The Capitana returned to the front of the fleet and set the armada's course for Havana once again.

Part II

La Florida

1715

Chapter 5

Vera Cruz was a small shanty town that only came alive when the fleets arrived to sell their goods, unload the mercury for the silver mines, and pick up the King's silver. During the past two hundred years, billions of pesos had been funneled through this obscure hole in the wall to the King's treasury in Spain. [1]

The New Spain Armada commanded by General Ubilla had been at Vera Cruz for two years. General Ubilla's fleet had originally consisted of eight ships when it left Seville for Vera Cruz in 1713. Several large storms diminished the fleet to only four ships during the two years with repairs to the existing vessels taking longer than expected.

The last storm had occurred in March, 1715 when hurricane winds struck Vera Cruz and hurled twelve ships against the coast. Ubilla's Capitana was driven onto a reef but the Almiranta was in protected waters and escaped undamaged. It took five weeks to refloat and repair the Capitana and finally in May, 1715 the fleet was ready to sail back to Spain. [9]

"Captain, ship on the horizon," the quartermaster shouted to Captain Moreno from the helm of the Capitana.

"A King's ship," Moreno thought to himself as he looked through his scope and then made his way to the helm.

"Quartermaster, let me know when the launch is put into the water. I'll let the General know of the ships arrival!" Moreno ordered.

Captain Moreno let the General know of the approaching ship and then waited at the railing for the launch to arrive.

"Captain Aldao, welcome aboard, I hope you had a safe journey," Moreno said as he greeted the Captain who he knew from the last war.

"Long and exhausting journey, but thankfully a safe one. It's good to see you again, is the General here?" Captain Aldao asked.

"Follow me Captain, he is awaiting your arrival," Moreno said showing the Captain the way to the Generals quarters.

"General, Captain Aldao is here to see you," Moreno said as he turned and exited the Generals quarters.

"General, it's good to see you again, I have a letter from the King and it's most urgent," Captain Aldao said as he gave the letter to the General.

"Captain, please pour yourself some wine while I read," General Ubilla said as he rose from his chair, opened the letter, and began reading.

"The war is over and Spain is broke. I guess the King is wondering what we have been doing over here for two years," General Ubilla thought out loud as he finished reading the letter.

"General, the King took all of the remaining treasure in the royal coffers and distributed it to various churches and monasteries throughout Spain for the saying of masses to insure the safe arrival of your fleet. It is a grave situation," Captain Aldao said solemnly.

"Captain, we have had many problems including a hurricane that sank four of our ships and damaged the Capitana.

Anyway, we are now ready to sail," the General said confidently as he sat down and poured more wine for the both of them.

"And did you receive word of the Queens dowry?" Captain Aldao asked as he raised his glass to drink.

"Yes, it arrived last week. Everything is here that the King asked for and it is magnificent," the General replied as he also raised his glass to drink.

"Salute, General," Captain Aldao said as he raised his glass higher.

"Salute, Captain," the general said and did likewise.

General Ubilla's fleet sailed the next month and rendezvoused with General Echeverz's fleet in Havana. General Ubilla told General Echeverz of his meeting with Captain Aldao and the urgency in getting the King's silver and the Queen's dowry to Spain as quickly as possible and General Echeverz told General Ubilla of the situation involving the Peruvian silver.

At a meeting of all the ship's captains most of the officers agreed that their ships were ready to sail. The word went out that the fleet would set sail near the end of July, even though several captains were hesitant about the weather and possible storms. Hurricanes were a serious threat to the fleets during this time of the year, but all the captains knew that the fleet was already late in getting the King's silver to Spain.

The combined fleet of twelve ships, including the two Capitanas and the two Almirantas, sailed out of the Havana harbor on July 27, 1715. The twelve ships had a combined cargo valued at 14,000,000 pesos in gold, silver, and emeralds. It was a spectacular sight as all the ships let go their main sails and headed for the Straits of Florida. [1,7]

The children and the other passengers were excited about getting underway and returning to their families in Spain. After two days of sailing under fair winds, everyone was in good spirits and thankful to finally be on their way to Seville.

Carmen could see most of the ships of the Armada as she scanned the horizon, their white sails extended fully from the steady southeast wind.

On the third day, Carmen noticed that the waves were growing larger even though the weather was clear and there was no storm in sight.

"Father Francisco, have you noticed how long and high the waves are this morning?" Carmen asked the priest as she watched the large waves rolling past the ship.

"It is beautiful my child, usually the large waves come from a storm further out to sea and hopefully it will not affect us," Father Francisco said hoping that the armada would be able to outrun the distant storm.

During the day the waves kept increasing in size and the wind started blowing harder out of the southeast. It was a good wind for the ships as they made their way up the Florida Straits.

General Ubilla, the officers, and the seasoned seaman all recognized the signs of an approaching storm. The General ordered all ships to lay on maximum sail in hopes that they could outrun the worst of the onslaught. But the ships were all heavy with cargo and at the most, could only sail at three to five knots.

That night the wind strengthened from the east and the waves grew larger. Sails were trimmed, hatches were closed, and loose gear restrained as the wind screamed through the rigging and the waves broke over the bow.

General Echeverz's Capitana plunged and rose in the rough sea as sailors climbed the main mast and braved the wind and the sea to furl the topsails.

"Maria, Maria, where are Juan and Father Francisco?" Carmen yelled to Maria who was grasping a yardarm and watching the wave's crash about the ship.

"Armando has ordered all passengers to go to their personal quarters, we need to find Juan and Father Francisco and let them know," Carmen shouted to be heard above the roaring wind.

"They went below to help the women and children find safer quarters," Maria said barely hanging on as a large wave crashed over the railing.

"Maria we need to get inside, Juan and Father Francisco will come to the cabin when they finish helping the others," Carmen said as she grabbed Maria's hand and headed for the cabin.

Everyone in the armada now realized that they were in the middle of a tumultuous storm. The winds were screaming, the waves were approaching twenty to thirty feet high, ships masts were starting to be toppled, and all the ships were being blown west to the Florida coast.

The Capitana took a direct hit from a large wave that crashed down on the ship's deck and cracked the main mast. The mast then fell to the deck and the ship shook violently upon impact as Juan and Father Francisco made their way back to their cabin.

The passengers were terrified when the water started rushing in as the ship was tossed about in the boiling sea of white foam and treacherous waves.

Carmen huddled in fear with Juan and Maria in their cabin as Father Francisco prayed for mercy on the passengers and crew.

All the ships by now had dropped their anchors in hopes of slowing their advance towards the Florida coast and certain destruction.

One of the merchant ships had lost its rudder and was headed straight for Echeverz's Capitana. The Capitana was helpless to maneuver out of its way in the raging wind and enormous waves.

The merchant ship bore down on the Capitana and the next wave slammed the merchant ship onto the Capitana's bow. Both ships were mortally wounded and started taking on water, the merchant ship lost most of its bow and the crew and passengers jumped for their lives to swim away from the sinking ship.

The Capitana was listing on its side but still afloat. Some of the crew and passengers ran for the water pumps while others threw everything they could find into the breached hull of the ship.

Carmen, Maria, Juan, and Father Francisco had run to the main deck after the two ships had collided. They all joined the others in throwing wood debris and sails into the breach to stop the water from gushing in.

It was of no use, the water could not be stopped, General Echeverz knew that the ship would slip beneath the waves in a matter of minutes.

At that moment, the ship suddenly stopped and shook violently as its hull hit a reef. On the next wave, the Capitana rose up, turned half way around and hit a second reef. The ship was stuck fast, the Capitana had found land.

Father Francisco and the children were thrown onto the deck by the sudden impact. It was difficult to stand as the waves crashed over the hull and onto the deck.

All the passengers were yelling and screaming, running to find something that they could use to swim to shore.

Father Francisco and Juan tied a rope around an empty water barrel and told Maria and Carmen to hold onto the rope as they pushed them and the barrel into the heavy surf. Father Francisco pried loose a deck plank from the stern and told Juan to hold onto it as they both jumped into the boiling madness.

Mercy was asked for and mercy was given a thousand times that night. The children and Father Francisco were spared as they were finally able to lose the grip of the strong current that tried to pull them back out to sea.

The night seemed to last forever. Carmen and Maria were wet, cold and scared as they tried to survive without shelter or fire. Father Francisco and Juan spent the night struggling in the surf to help survivors trying to reach the beach.

The morning found groups of survivors stranded together on the beach, still trying to shield themselves from the high winds and blinding sand. The beach was littered with cargo, ship wreckage, and the bodies of the passengers and crew who had drowned in the storm. Amidst the carnage, Carmen, Maria and Juan huddled together, thankful that they had survived.

Wreck of the 1715 Spanish Armada

The 1715 Spanish Armada, consisting of two combined fleets of twelve ships, all wrecked save one on the eastern coast of Florida from Sebastian down to Saint Lucie. General Juan Esteban de Ubilla's fleet consisted of five ships and General Don

Antonio Echeverz's fleet consisted of seven ships. All of the wrecked ships were sunk or grounded by the hurricane near or on the shore with their treasure of 14,000,000 pesos in silver and gold buried beneath the waves. [1,7,8]

General Ubilla, General Echeverz, and half of the fleets crew and passengers had perished in the storm. Women and children had little chance of surviving if they had been swept over the ship's rails and into the waves that were exploding all about them. Even if they had made it close to shore the waves and currents were so fierce that only the strongest could elude their grasp. [1,7,8]

General Ubilla's Fleet

Capitana Nuestra Senora de la Regla

General Ubilla's Capitana was the lead ship ballasted at 471 tons, armed with 50 cannons, and carrying 1,386 chests filled with 2,559,917 pesos in silver coins, gold bars, gifts and worked silver. The Capitana struck a reef 1800 feet from shore, losing some ballast and a few cannons before grounding on the next reef, 700 feet from shore in 12 feet of water. "General Ubilla and 225 of his crew and passengers perished in the raging seas." The huge waves smashed against her sides until the bow separated and she came apart 6 miles to the south of where Ubilla's Almiranta wrecked. [1,7,8,9]

Almiranta Santo Cristo de San Roman

Admiral Don Francisco Salmon was aboard General Ubilla's Almiranta that was ballasted at 450 tons and armed with 54 cannons. The Almiranta carried 990 chests filled with 2,687,416 pesos in silver and gold and 85 chests of gifts (emeralds?). Across from the Sebastian River, the Almiranta hit the third reef out and then grounded on the second reef, 900 feet offshore. The impact at the third reef tore the stern apart and split open the hull, scattering hundreds of chests filled with silver and gold across the ocean floor. A letter from Admiral Salmon to the King on September 20, 1715, said "The second time the ship hit the reef the ship broke into three pieces. The center of the ship stayed below water, but the bow and stern were thrown closer to shore, which was responsible for saving most of the people. However, 82 drowned, and at the distance of two leagues, four hours earlier, the General and over 200 persons drowned." [1,7,8,9]

Refuerzo NuestraSenora de la Concepcion
Urca de Lima

The *Urca de Lima* was the refuerzo or supply ship for General Ubilla's fleet and was ballasted at 350 tons with twenty cannons. The *Urca* carried 252,171 pesos of silver, 136 chests of gifts (emeralds?), 13 chests of worked silver, 32 chests of porcelain K'ang His, and brazil wood. The *Urca* avoided total disintegration by being able to anchor in 18 feet of water between two reefs at the mouth of a river. However, the next day a second storm came through and sank her in shallow water but still leaving the deck above the water line. [1,7,8.9]

Patache Nuestra Senora de las Nieves

The *Nuestra Senora de las Nieves* was the patache for General Ubilla's fleet and ballasted at 195 tons with 12 cannons. The *Nieves* carried 44,000 pesos in silver, 58 chests of gifts (emeralds?), 7 chests of chinese porcelain, along with tanned hides, indigo, and brazil wood. The *Nieves* was destroyed by the waves of the hurricane with her cargo, passengers and crew scattered along the beach to the south of a river's mouth. "Two dozen drowned as the deck lifted off the hull, but some one hundred survivors rode the wreckage ashore like a raft." [1,7,8,9]

General Echeverz's Fleet

Capitana Nuestra Senora del Carmen

General Don Antonio de Echeverz y Zubiza selected the *Nuestra Senora del Carmen*, having just recently been built, as his Capitania because of her size. The 1,072 ton *Carmen* had 52 cannons and like all the ships in Echeverz's fleet she was under contract with the King to pick up the treasure and return it to Seville. The registered treasure onboard the *Carmen* was 79,967 pesos in gold bars and 1,175 pesos of silver. During the hurricane the *Carmen* lost her mast and steerage before striking the second reef 900 feet offshore and sinking on her starboard side in 19 feet of water. "Despite the nearness of the beach, the General and 113 others perish." [1,7,8,9]

1715

Almiranta Nuestra Senora del Rosario

General Echeverz's Almiranta, the *Nuestra Senora del Rosario*, was ballasted at 312 tons and armed with 40 cannons. The Almiranta was loaded with 15,514 pesos in gold bars along with brazil wood, leather hides and tobacco when she departed Havana. The Almiranta was blown northward by the hurricane winds until she struck an outer reef in 28 feet of water, losing many of her cannon and disintegrating towards the beach. "*Rosario* was totally destroyed and 124 passengers and crew including Echeverz's son, were drowned." [1,7,8,9]

Patache Nuestra Senora de la Concepcion

The *Nuestra Senora de la Concepcion* was the Patache for General Echeverz's fleet and ballasted at 256 tons with 32 cannon (18 ten-pounders, 10 six-pounders, and 4 four-pounders). The *Concepcion* had a crew of 136 and carried 4,714 pesos in silver, 3,000 pesos in gold, along with tanned hides, cacao, and brazil wood. The day of the hurricane the *Concepcion* was last seen heading north "...the ship *Concepcion*, which was wrecked at Cape Canaveral, had only seven survivors who, after great hardship, finally reached shore." [1,7,8,9]

Refuerzo San Miguel

General Echeverz's Refuerzo was the *San Miguel* carrying 750 tons of tobacco and a quantity of silver plate that was loaded in Havana. The *San Miguel* was a Spanish built ship ballasted at 180 tons with 22 cannons (eighteen 4 pounders and four 2 pounders) and owned by General Echeverz. The day before the hurricane struck, the *San Miguel* was north of the fleet. Admiral Salmon wrote to the King on September 20, 1715 that "there is little doubt that they sank on the high seas, and this is proven because fragments of a ship or ships were found on the north coast of Saint Augustine." [1,7,8]

Nuestra Senora de la Popa

The *Nuestra Senora de la Popa* was a captured Dutch sloop which General Echeverz purchased for 2,000 pesos in Portabello. Echeverz put *Juan Baptista Zalema* on board as captain plus a first mate, a pilot, and fifteen crew members. The *Popa* had probably been loaded with tobacco at Havana and was shattered by the waves of the hurricane as it was washed ashore near Echeverz's Capitana and Almiranta. [1,7,8]

El Ciervo

General Echeverz also purchased another vessel in Portobello that was larger than the *Popa* and could carry considerably more cargo. It was a French vessel named the *El Ciervo* that cost 4,125 pesos and captained by *Salvador Costan*. The *El Ciervo* was probably heavily loaded with tobacco at Havana and "disappeared somewhere in deep water with no survivors." [1,7,8]

John S. Potter wrote that General Ubilla's Capitana *"broke her bottom on the seaward edge of the outermost reef, spilling ballast and heavy cargo onto the coral and the sand floor*

30 feet below. The lightened hull was carried in over the reef by surging mountains of water, then across the middle coral barrier into a sand trough less than 100 feet wide separating the two innermost reefs. Here it disintegrated. Most of the cannons and lading spilled out onto the sand, only 15 feet deep and 300 feet from shore. A trail of gold, silver, and jewelry stretched inshore for 700 feet across coral and sand from the ballast." [1]

Potter concluded that *"the four Capitana's and Almiranta's carried 14,000,000 pesos in registered treasure. Since the armada's departure from the New World had been delayed a full year, contraband cargo was crammed onto its ships. An estimate published in 1868 by Jacobo de Pezuela valued the total cargo at 65,000,000 pesos."* (a peso at this time equaled one troy ounce of silver) [1]

Chapter 6

Carmen could not imagine a more desolate and unforgiving fate. The shipwrecked survivors were castaways, a long way from the comfort of their homes and families and the only thing on their minds was finding their valuables and being rescued.

Since this fleet was one of the richest in treasure from the new world in many years, it only made sense that the King of Spain would try to recover his silver as quickly as possible.

"But how long would it take for Spanish ships to reach them? What about the pyrates that prey on the treasure fleets? As soon as they hear, it'll be like bees to honey," Carmen thought to herself.

No one was taking command on the beach and it was chaos with the survivors fighting for what little provisions that had been deposited on shore by the storm.

Carmen was walking the beach helping to look for survivors among the many dead who had been washed ashore after the storm. She knelt down beside a passenger lying motionless to see if there was still any life. She saw that there was none and as she rose up she felt the presence of someone behind her.

She turned and faced a young woman who, just hours before, had barely survived death and looked like she was going to collapse.

"Can you help me find my daughter?" the woman asked with a soft raspy voice.

"Of course I will," Carmen replied.

They set off down the beach cautiously checking the bodies they came across but none of them had survived. Others were out checking also, looking for relatives or seeing what they could take from the dead.

Carmen thought about Armando and asked several people if they had seen the Captain. One old man, who looked like he was about to take his last breath, said that he had seen the Captain out in the surf and when he looked back he was gone.

"Sharks, sharks are everywhere, devouring the dead bodies," the old man cried out as he looked beyond the waves and watched as the fins swam through the water and then dove out of sight.

As they were making their way back to where Juan and Maria were, the young woman pointed at the breaking waves.

"Do you see the child being swept in by the waves?" the woman said.

"Yes, I see," Carmen replied.

They waited for several minutes until the child was close to shore, then Carmen and the woman waded out and grabbed her away from the waves. As they were pulling the child to shore the woman began to cry. The dead child was her daughter and Carmen recognized her as the little girl who helped her sell the tickets on board the ship. She like most of the children on the ships had perished.

The passengers who did not lose their lives were in danger of losing everything that they had worked for in the new world. For many of them, returning to Spain without their accrued wealth would be out of the question.

Carmen rejoined Maria and Juan and they all three searched for their chests on the beach and along the shore. When they could not find them, they went to the spot on the beach that was closest to the wreck of the Capitana.

General Echeverz's Capitana was lying on the bottom, about 900 feet from the beach with its stern barely showing above the waterline. The passengers who had gathered at the Capitana knew that their fortunes were deep inside the sunken ship and that they would have to risk their lives to get them back.

The Capitana survivors all agreed that they could not wait for help. They were in danger of losing their valuables to pyrates or even worst to the natives that were described as fierce warriors who favored Spanish silver.

Stories were many about the natives who lived in the jungle beyond the beach who captured shipwrecked survivors and kept them as slaves or worse.

Father Francisco pleaded with the survivors to wait for the Spanish ships to arrive with divers who could salvage the sunken ships much quicker and safer than the untrained passengers. For the survivors to try and find their chests in the ship's hull would be dangerous work, sense without warning the ship's decks could collapse and trap those below.

The survivors did not heed the Father's warning and went to work making a diving platform from the ship's wreckage that they found on the beach. The diving raft proved to be seaworthy and the survivors were able to row it out to the stern of the Capitana that was lying in about 16 feet of water.

The bravest and most physically fit of the men were promised rewards from the wealthy survivors to retrieve their fortunes from the hull of the sunken ship. The men started diving from the raft and when a chest was found, ropes were secured and the chests were hauled aboard the floating platform.

The divers worked late into the evening until they could no longer avoid the large sharks that had gathered around the shipwreck. The survivors and divers then rowed the platform ashore where the divers received their compensation and the survivors who were fortunate enough, took possession of their chests.

However, the elation over the recovery of the survivors valuables was soon dampened by the coming of night and with it the scourge of the jungle. Everyone buried themselves in the sand with a handkerchief or piece of cloth over their head so they could breathe and avoid the onslaught. Even with this defensive measure the hundreds of thousands of mosquitos were still able to find their target.

With each passing day more and more chests were retrieved from their watery grave, giving hope to the desperate survivors who were quickly running out of fresh water. Aware that natives inhabited the lands beyond the beach, several small groups of the survivors armed themselves with whatever weapons they could find and set out to find water.

Juan had chosen to be a diver so he could earn money from the survivors while at the same time looking for the two chests containing their father's gold. After several days Juan had been able to help retrieve many of the survivor's chests but so far had not been able to locate the family chests.

Two days later, in the evening when the sharks started to feed, everyone was encouraging the divers to work longer for more compensation. Juan and two other divers wanted the additional silver pesos and agreed to make several more dives.

Diving down, Juan and the other two divers made their way to the collapsed stern of the ship. Looking for any sign of his cabin, Juan pushed further into the stern's wreckage avoiding any beam that looked too weak or about to break from the strain. Juan spotted several chests that could be lifted through the wreckage and as he got closer he recognized his father's initials on the brass lock of one of the chests.

Quickly the divers lashed the rope around the chest and made for the surface. On board the raft, everyone pulled to set the chest free. They had brought it half way through the stern when a wooden beam snapped from the pressure and landed on the front of the chest, breaking the lock open.

The chest was still in-tact but the beam blocked its path from being pulled out. Juan immediately jumped in and found the beam heavy but moveable. A large tiger shark cruised overhead and Juan wasted no time in pushing the beam out of the way.

Returning to the raft, Juan and the divers pulled as hard as they could to bring the heavy chest to the surface. As the chest broke free from the stern, the ropes gave way and the lid opened spilling all of the gold onto the ocean floor. Juan didn't panic for he knew that it would take only a few dives to recover their gold but because of the sharks it would have to wait until the next day.

The divers paddled the raft to shore, unloaded the chests and collected their commission from the grateful survivors. Juan was able to trade some of his silver for fish with survivors who had killed them with handmade spears.

"Good news, we have dinner. It's not much, but better than nothing," Juan said as he handed the fish to Carmen and sat down next to the fire.

"How did the diving go? Did you find our chests?" Carmen asked as she started to clean the fish.

"I found one but the lock came off as we were pulling it up and it's now on the ocean floor," Juan said as Maria let out a gasp.

"Don't worry, it will be easy to retrieve, first thing in the morning I will be able to bring it all up to the surface," Juan said confidently.

"At least we know where it's at," Carmen said as she began to cut the fish into strips.

"Is there any word about the men who went searching for water," Juan asked.

"None, it's been almost two days now and people are thinking that the natives might have found them," Father Francisco said as he helped to put the fish on sticks.

"We must find water in the next few days or we all will be in trouble," Juan said as he took some of the fish from Father Francisco and held it over the fire to cook.

Everyone knew that without water they would soon perish, Juan decided that diving for their gold would have to wait, finding water for his sisters was more important.

The next morning Juan and a few of the crew and passengers gathered weapons and set out in the direction that the first group had taken. The night before, Carmen and Maria had cut pieces of rope for Juan to tie onto trees so the men could find their way back to the beach.

As they moved deeper into the jungle, Juan started tying a piece of rope to a tree limb or bush every twenty to thirty feet. Unfortunately, it was useless because the natives had found their trail and were collecting the pieces of rope as they followed them.

Not having machetes was making it extremely difficult for the survivors to cut their way through the dense jungle, causing their pace to be punishingly slow. They continued on, fighting the thick jungle undergrowth, until they finally reached a clearing where they found themselves surrounded by the natives.

While the natives kept their spears and arrows aimed at the hearts of the survivors, two of the natives grabbed Juan, bound his hands, and forced him down to the ground.

On his knees with the natives yelling at him, Juan surely must have thought that these were his last moments on earth. One native tossed down the rope ties in front of him and started yelling into his face.

Whatever they were upset about it did not look good for Juan and he began to pray. Just as Juan finished praying, a loud blast from a rifle pierced his ears and sent the screaming native to meet his god.

The other natives vanished into the jungle as quickly as they had appeared. Shouts of joy exploded from the survivors as the first group of survivors who had sought water emerged from behind the rocks and trees.

Carlos, General Echeverz's first mate, untied Juan and explained that they had narrowly escaped from being captured by the natives and eventually they had found water. The two groups made their way to where the water was located, filled all their water containers, and then started making their way back to the beach.

As they emerged from the jungle and approached the beach they expected a jubilant return, instead they saw many of the survivors hurriedly trying to bury their chests in the sand. One of the survivors shouted pyrates and the group checked their weapons and raced for the beach.

Behind a sand dune, Juan and the others witnessed pyrates forcing the survivors to carry their chests to their longboats on the beach. Juan spotted his two sisters and Father Francisco struggling to carry a chest that was destined to be loaded onto a longboat and rowed out to a ship anchored just offshore.

Juan and Carlos spoke quickly and then shared their plan with the rest of the group. Hiding their weapons under their clothes, the group split up and one by one they made their way to the side of their fellow survivors.

As soon as the pyrate's longboats were loaded, half of the pyrate's started rowing their longboats out to their ship leaving the other pyrate's to guard the survivors. When the pyrate's longboats reached the ship, Juan and Carlos gave the signal and the group of survivors lifted their weapons and aimed them at the remaining pyrates. The pyrates responded in kind and most of them were blown away where they stood.

When the pyrate's on the ship heard the shots fired, they loaded the stolen chests onto the ship's deck, tied the longboats to the ship, and set sail as the remaining captured pyrates on shore swore revenge on those who were leaving them behind.

Chapter 7

Juan and Carlos conveyed to the crowd of survivors exactly how they found the water and then how the encounter with the natives turned deadly. All of the survivors now realized that they were in a grave situation of losing not only their valuables but also their lives as well. The pyrates and the natives now knew that a fleet of ships had been forced onto the shores of Florida.

The pyrates would probably bring back more ships, the natives were probably not happy about losing one of their tribe members, and waiting for the Spanish salvage ships to arrive was fast not becoming an option.

Carlos said that the pyrates could probably return with more ships in about five to seven days. If they dived for their chests over the next three or four days and then traveled to the north they might be able to escape their assault. There would still be the threat from the natives but they stood a better chance of fighting them off rather than facing another attack by the pyrates.

That night Juan and Carlos shared their trek into the jungle with Carmen, Maria, and Father Francisco as they ate fish and sat around the fire. Carmen and Maria were fascinated by Juan's description of the natives and they thanked Carlos for saving their brother from an early grave.

The next morning the divers made their way out to the Capitana and started bringing up chests from the sunken ship. Juan dove for their gold and was able to find almost all of it at the spot where it had falling to the ocean floor. It took Juan many dives to bring it all to the surface and on one of the last dives he found several rings and pieces of jewelry belonging to Carmen and Maria that they cherished as gifts from their parents.

After two days of diving, Juan and the other divers were exhausted and knew that they could not possibly get everyone's chest to the surface before the pyrates returned. Obtaining the assistance of the captured pyrates to bring up the chests could be a possible solution. The divers sent a proposal to the pyrates and that night the pyrates sent word back to Juan and Carlos that they wanted to talk.

"Speaking for the crew, I would like to make an offer to help everyone recover their sunken valuables." Louis LaTortue said with a heavy French accent.

"Go on, let us know your proposition," Carlos replied.

"Our freedom first and then fifty percent of the recovered wealth," Louis offered.

"Freedom yes, but fifty percent no," Carlos replied laughing at the preposterous suggestion.

"We will be risking our lives with the sharks. Surely it must be worth that much to the passengers?" Louis challenged.

Carlos knew not to trust the pyrates but the survivors were in a tight spot, more pyrates would be returning in a few days and they didn't know when the King's ships would arrive.

At the same time, Louis and his crew knew that upon the arrival of the Spanish ships that their lives would not be worth much more than the sand under there feet.

"The passengers have offered twenty-five percent and not one percent more," Carlos replied.

"Done," Louis replied and extended his hand.

Louis and his crew worked like dogs to lift the chests from the ship for their lives depended on it. They knew that they needed to move quickly to bring as many chests as possible to the surface, collect their share of the passenger's wealth, and then leave before the Spanish ships showed up. After two days, the pyrate's raised most of the survivor's chests and the survivors had buried what they could not take with them.

Carmen and Maria found a spot near the base of a sand dune to bury their father's gold and the next morning everyone awoke to strong winds and dark clouds blowing in from the southeast.

The survivors could wait no longer, fearing that either the pyrates or the natives would soon be returning, they headed north along the beach. Louis and his crew, with their commission in hand, decided to head north with the survivors to see if any other ships like Echeverz's Capitana had wrecked close to shore.

As night approached, the survivors of the Capitana and the pyrates reached one of the ships of the Ubilla fleet that had grounded near the shore. They searched for survivors, but no one was to be found. It was clear that if anyone survived this wreck, they must have headed north for the fort at St. Augustine.

Weary from the days march, everyone found a place on the beach and collapsed. Most buried themselves in the sand and fell to sleep, while others built fires for protection against the mosquitos. The pyrates laid claim to the shipwreck and its cargo and planned to start salvage at first light.

The next morning everyone awoke to Juan and Carlos yelling out the names of Carmen and Maria. Juan and Carlos had awakened and found the girls missing from their camp. They went from group to group on the beach asking about the girl's whereabouts, but no one had heard anything during the night. Most had slept soundly, exhausted by the previous days march, and would not have awoken unless cannons were being fired.

While Juan and Carlos searched the beach, Carmen and Maria were being dragged through the jungle like animals. They were beaten and pushed along the trail by fierce natives, who were short, muscular, and hardened by their primitive existence.

The girls were exhausted and every time they fell the natives wacked their legs with sticks. Carmen pleaded with the natives to stop and let them rest but the natives did not understand nor care what they were trying to tell them.

Juan knew that it must have been the natives who took his sisters. Everyone searched the beach and the dunes until one of the men found tracks and a ripped piece of cloth.

"It's from Maria's dress," Juan said.

Carlos brought everyone together and asked for volunteers to search for the girls. Getting no response from any of the survivors, Juan offered two gold bars to each man who journeyed with them. Two of the survivors who could not find their chests and three of the ship's crew members gladly agreed to join the search. The seven men collected their weapons and started following the trail that led into the jungle.

The natives had reached their village with the girls barely alive and their bodies riddled with cuts and bruises. Thrown into a thatched hut and tied to the center post both girls were almost to the point of hysteria, not knowing what the natives intended to do with them.

Carlos acted as point man with the other men following, fending off mosquitos, snakes, and insects as best they could. Stopping at a stream, the men covered their faces and hands with mud that gave them relief from the blood sucking pests. It wasn't difficult for Carlos to keep on the trail, the natives and the girls left footprints, pieces of cloth and blood. Carlos noticed that the blood was increasing and quickened his pace to catch up to them.

It was growing dark and the girls could hear angry voices outside the hut getting louder and louder until it was just two men shouting at each other. Whether to be slaved or sacrificed was usually the contention for disagreement among the natives.

The shouting stopped and two natives entered the hut, untied the girls and shoved them into the center of the village. There they were tied to a stake next to a burning fire where all the villagers had gathered. Several natives had started dancing about the fire and soon most of the villagers joined them either singing or dancing to the steady beat of drums.

Carlos and Juan could hear the drums in the distance and quickly made their way through the jungle until they reached the edge of the village.

As the men approached quietly they saw the natives dancing about the fire but not Carmen and Maria. They waited in place to see what would happen next, a shout from the crowd and the natives dropped to their knees.

Carlos and Juan could then see Carmen and Maria tied to a stake near the fire and then a large native caked in red mud exited a hut in front of the fire.

The native had a large ax in his right hand and slowly raised it as he approached the girls. As the native raised the ax above his head a shot rang out from Juan's rifle and the bullet pierced the native's skull.

As the native dropped dead from the bullet that blew off most of his skull, the other natives scattered like chickens, running in all directions. Juan rushed in to untie the girls and everyone followed Carlos back into the jungle, running for their lives. They ran until they were out of breath, stopping to make sure everyone was still together.

They were in thick jungle and even with moon light it was still pitch black. Some wanted to wait for mornings light to determine which way to go but Carlos warned against staying too close to the village.

They found a path and made good time along it until they felt safe enough to stop. They moved off the path a short distance and huddled together, fighting off the insects and mosquitoes, not knowing what or when to expect retaliation.

Morning light brought apprehension about moving out. No one had really slept, it was either worrying about the natives coming or fighting off the insects. They cautiously crawled out of their hiding place and started moving towards the sunrise.

They were still in thick jungle, the hard blades of grass cut into their arms and legs which bled and attracted flies. The going was slow but so far there was no sign of the natives. By noon they were all exhausted from having to make their way through the thick jungle undergrowth and with the lack of food and water they were starting to show signs of dehydration.

Stopping at a stream for water, they caught their breath and argued over which direction to go. The sun was straight overhead and it was difficult to keep an easterly bearing in the middle of the jungle.

One of the ship's crewmen saw a fallen coconut and as he reached to pick it up, an arrow caught him in the stomach. Another crewman reached out to help him and a spear pierced his heart and he was dead before he hit the ground.

Two natives advanced with bows drawn and each one caught a bullet from the rifles of Carlos and Juan. The other crewman helped the wounded man stand up and then they started moving away from the natives. The survivors followed them, traveling a short distance and then taking a defensive position to wait for another attack.

It never came. They waited for a few minutes and then moved in the opposite direction of the sun. After several hours of slow progress through the thick bush they came on a clearing in the jungle, it was the first of many to come as they continued east towards the beach.

The thick bush and clearings soon evolved into large open areas of tall grass with streams and waterways meandering through them. This was alligator country where female alligators built their nests high above the water line but still had easy access to the larger bodies of water where they hunted for food.

The survivors were not familiar with an alligators hunting technique and did not know how fiercely territorial they were. They trekked on through the open swamp, seeing only one or two alligators with fortunately no critical encounters.

It was getting dark when they finally started to hear the faint sound of crashing waves on the beach. They were ecstatic at the thought of being out of the jungle and away from the natives.

But Carlos was cautious "let's check it out before we go running onto the beach, it's been two days since we left and there is no telling what has happened," Carlos warned.

"I'll go ahead to scout and return as soon as I see what the situation is." Carlos said as he started to make his way towards the beach.

Carlos soon returned and told the others that the survivors had left and that the pyrates were on the beach near the shipwreck.

"The seaman passed away while you were gone, it's now only the eight of us," Juan said. "We can't wait here forever let's go take a look and see what we can do."

"It's almost dark and there's nothing we can do except endure the mosquitos and wait for morning to decide," Carlos replied.

They all agreed and each one dug a hole in the sand, about the size of their bodies, and covered themselves in sand. It was miserable but better than being eating alive by the blood thirsty mosquitos and biting flies.

They awoke with the sunrise, extremely hungry but with serious business to attend too.

"Everyone stay where you are, check to make sure your guns are loaded and ready to fire. Carlos and I will be back in a short time," Juan said as he and Carlos prepared to move towards the beach.

Just as Juan and Carlos reached the first set of dunes in front of the beach they spotted a ship coming from the north and sailing close to shore. They saw the pyrates back away from the shipwreck and then run for the nearest sand dune. After reaching the dune they all crouched down as if trying to hide from the approaching ship.

"It must be the pyrate ship that left Louis and the others stranded when we captured them. But why do they run from the pyrates on the ship?" Jaun asked bewildered by the reaction of Louis and his crew.

1715

Chapter 8

Threatened by Captain Vane and in hopes of saving their lives, some of the survivors of General Echeverz's Capitana had told Vane of General Ubilla's Capitana.

The survivors told Vane that there were two Capitana's and that it was Ubilla's Capitana that was carrying the most treasure along with the Queen's dowry in jewels, gold and silver.

They then told Vane that Ubilla's Capitana was leading the Armada and that it must be located to the north of where they had shipwrecked. [7,10]

After losing one-third of his crew on the beach at General Echeverz's Capitana, Captain Vane sailed north to an area where he thought Ubilla's Capitana might have wrecked. They soon spotted wreckage from a ship with passenger belongings scattered for almost a mile up and down the beach.

The surviving passengers and crew of the wreck were all clustered together in several different groups along the beach. Some of them began waving when they saw Captain Vane's ship approaching until they realized it was not a Spanish ship. Captain Vane had his black flag raised and nothing more was heard from the castaways.

Captain Vane put out most of his crew in two longboats. Using grappling hooks, the ship and the two longboats swept the waters starting near the shore, hoping to hook onto any part of the shipwreck.

"Captain, we have something," Mr. England shouted out to Captain Vane from the second longboat.

"Well done, Mr. England," Captain Vane shouted back. Vane thought highly of Mr. England's capabilities as quartermaster but kept a close eye out for any sign of discontent.

Captain Vane ordered the ship turned to where Mr. England was located and the other longboat joined them. The crew took ship's planking and laid it across both longboats and lashed it down so that the two longboats made a floating platform.

Mr. England then ordered two of the crew to dive down to see what they hooked. They surfaced a few minutes later, grinning from ear to ear.

"It's part of the stern and there are chests of silver spilled over the wreck," one of the divers shouted out.

The other diver confirmed that it was only half of the lower stern.

"Mr. England, you continue to work this site and I will look for the other part of the stern," Captain Vane shouted as he walked to the helm and ordered his crew to throw out the grappling hooks once clear of the wreck site.

After making only two sweeps of the area, one of the crew hooked onto something solid. "Drop the anchor!" Vane ordered as everyone ran to the port side of the ship.

"Emanuel and Philippe, over the side," Vane ordered as his two best divers dove from the ship into the water.

"It's the other part of the stern," Emanuel shouted out after he and Philippe had surfaced.

"Dive again and check to see if there are any chests to be seen," Vane shouted back.

Emanuel and Philippe dove back down about sixteen feet to where the other half of the stern lay on the first reef. The stern was split open and the divers could see into the structure.

"Yes Captain, there are chests, we need the ropes and hooks," Emanuel shouted after both divers had returned to the surface.

As the divers dove back towards the stern Emanuel caught a glimpse of a long shadow off in the distance but quickly returned his attention to the first chest that they saw.

The two divers worked quickly to hook and tie the wooden chest, barely getting back to the surface where they both were left gasping for air.

"Captain, the first chest is ready, it's from the Captain's quarters," Emanuel shouted out after regaining his strength.

"Hoist it up!" Emanuel shouted out to the crew.

"Careful as you go, gentlemen," Captain Vane warned. "We don't want our silver spread all over the ocean floor."

The crew tugged on the rope and could tell it was starting to move. They had to be ready for the drop to come when the chest would fall free from the cabin into the open water.

"Hold tight," Captain Vane ordered as the crew slid towards the railing when the chest dropped free in the water.

The chest was heavier than twenty cannon balls but the crew held tight the rope and started pulling the chest up from the shallow waters. Once the chest was at the waterline of the ship, two of the crew put grappling hooks on it to help pull it up and over the railing.

The crew pulled up three more chests from the Captain's cabin and then started working on the chests found below the Captain's quarters.

"Captain Vane, Mr. England is signaling for the third longboat to help row the platform to the ship," Mr. Langford said.

"Men, to the longboat and help Mr. England with our treasure," Captain Vane shouted out. "Mr. Langford, I'll be needing your help, so stay on board."

The men lowered the third longboat over the side and started rowing out to where Mr. England and the rest of the crew were waiting to be towed.

"Mr. Langford, I need your help to secure four of the chests," Captain Vane ordered as the crew in the longboat made their way to the longboat platform.

"We'll be keeping them in a safe place, separate from the others," Captain Vane said.

Captain Vane and Mr. Langford struggled putting the first four chests that were brought aboard from the stern of the shipwreck into Captain Vane's quarters.

"Blast it, it must be one of the new locking devices to keep us away from what is legally ours," Vane said as he fumbled around the chest looking for the opening to the lock.

"Captain, I've seen this before, I think I can open it," Mr. Langford declared.

"Then go ahead man and have at it," Vane ordered.

Mr. Langford had learned of this new type of invisible locking mechanism from Captain Vane's quartermaster, Mr. England. A hidden door on the lid of the chest had to be found and opened to reveal the trigger for the lock.

The top of the chest was crisscrossed with brass and wood that gave the appearance of a chess board. Mr. Langford began tapping each piece of wood, listening for a hollow sound. When he heard it, he pushed down on the piece of wood and slid the tiny door back to reveal the trigger for the lock.

"The chest has a trap door system, you have to find the right spot, like this, and then slide it back and the lock releases, like this," Mr. Langford said as he lifted the lid of the chest to reveal an almost unimaginable wealth in gold coins, jewelry, and emeralds.

Mr. Langford unlocked the other three chests and they found the same valuable cargo. After he closed and locked the chests, Vane turned to Mr. Langford.

"Mr. Langford, this will be just between you and I with an extra share for your consideration," Vane said as he gave Mr. Langford a slap on the back.

"Thank you Captain," Mr. Langford replied as Vane padlocked his cabin shut.

"Ahoy the ship," Mr. England shouted from his approaching longboat.

"Good work Mr. England," Vane said while eyeing the platform loaded with chests.

"How many chests did you find on the wreck?" Vane asked.

"Enough to make everyone filthy rich and pay off the Governor of Port Royal for clemency," Mr. England shouted back as the platform was moved into position alongside the ship.

The crew used rope and pulley to bring all the chests aboard and stored them below deck. The crew then rowed the platform to the port side of the ship and started diving on the part of the stern where Emanuel and Philippe had been working.

Emanuel and Philippe dived to help bring up many more chests until they again saw a long dark shadow lurking off in the distance.

"Captain, something is down there and it's starting to come closer to the stern," Emanuel shouted as he surfaced.

Emanuel looked back into the water just in time to see a large shark grab Philippe by the legs and drag him down.

"Captain, a shark took Philippe," Emanuel shouted out as Philippe's blood made its way to the surface.

"Everyone out of the water and be quick about it!" Captain Vane ordered.

All the divers left the water and the ship's crew lifted the last chest as Philippe's blood spread quickly about the ship.

"Captain with all the blood the sharks will be as thick as mosquitos," Mr. England said.

"Mr. England, get the men aboard and tie the longboats to the ship, we'll sail back to the first Capitana where there will hopefully be less sharks to contend with," Captain Vane ordered.

Chapter 9

Juan and Carlos moved back to where Carmen and the others were hiding behind a sand dune. As they did, they saw that Louis and his pyrates were heading straight their way.

"The pyrates are coming towards us, get your weapons ready," Juan said. "When I give the signal swing your weapons over the top of the dune and take aim at their hearts."

Louis and his crew continued moving towards them and then started up the sand dune where the survivors were waiting with cocked pistols and rifles.

"Stop and put your weapons down," Carlos demanded as the survivors aimed their weapons at the pyrates hearts.

"We want no blood," Louis said as they all laid their weapons on the sand.

"Come over quickly and sit down cross legged, hands on the sand in front of you," Carlos ordered. "We'll shoot the first pyrate that doesn't do what we say."

"We are not quite pyrates, yet," Louis said.

"What do you mean you are not quite pyrates?" Carlos asked.

"Captain Vane and his crew captured the merchant ship that we sailed on and he offered our crew the chance to join him as pyrates," Louis explained.

"We thought our chances would be better serving under Vane rather than being set adrift in a longboat," Louis said.

"What happened to the ship you were sailing on?" asked Carlos.

"Some of his men took control of the merchant ship and sailed it east and we joined Captain Vane to sail here for salvaging the Spanish silver," Louis said.

"That's why it didn't matter to him whether you lived or died when we captured you?" Carlos asked.

"Yes" Louis said. "Captain Vane has no soul, a treacherous man giving no quarter if need be to English, French or Spanish."

"Wait here," Carlos said as he grabbed Juan's arm and they moved to the bottom of the sand dune.

"I believe him, now what to do?" Carlos said.

"Walking north like the other survivor's means encountering more natives and perhaps more pyrates," Juan said.

"Waiting here for the Spanish ships means waiting for the natives to attack us again," Carlos said.

They paused, looked at each other, and in unison said, "the ship."

"If we could somehow get the ship away from Captain Vane, then we could sail for Havana," Carlos said.

"Louis and his crew could make that happen for us," Juan said.

"Let me do the talking," Carlos said as they moved back up the dune.

"Louis, we have a proposition, do you want to listen?" Carlos said.

"Go on," Louis said.

"We all work together to get the ship away from Captain Vane and sail to Havana," Carlos said.

"We would be hanged in Havana and what about the Spanish silver on his ship?" Louis replied.

"Captain Vane would not only seek revenge but when he found us he would make our deaths slow and agonizing," Louis warned.

"Our choices are limited, it's either the natives or Captain Vane who will be our demise," Juan said.

"What if we sailed to a neutral harbor and left the ship for Vane to reacquire," Carlos suggested.

"That could work," Louis said as he looked at his crew who were nodding approval.

"Then let's shake on this agreement and decide the next move," Carlos said as they shook hands and all gathered about.

"This will be dangerous but it's the only way" Louis warned. "Tonight they will all be drunk by midnight and that's when we can get aboard the ship."

"And then we attack?" Juan asked

"Not exactly," Louis replied "We hide in a safe place and at the right time we will strike and take the ship."

"What about sharks when we swim out to the ship?" Carlos asked.

"We will build baskets," Louis replied while grinning to his crew.

So they would be out of harm's way, Carmen, Maria, and the two survivors left immediately heading back south to General Echeverz's Capitana. Carrying their weapons and some water they would be there by nightfall and would find a safe place to wait for the captured ship to pick them up.

All the others started making three shark cages out of young tree limbs strapped together by vines in a basket shape. Placed in the water the shark cage floated with only the rim of the basket showing and accommodated three men who would kick out the back and swim it to Vane's ship.

"Captain Vane, you realize this is not the Capitana on which we were before?" Mr. England asked.

"Certainly, but this wreck is almost on shore and by the looks it has not been salvaged," Captain Vane replied as he ordered the crew into the longboats.

"Mr. England, we must make haste and get what we can before the Spanish salvage ships arrive. If there is time, then we will return to the Capitana when the sharks have calmed down," Captain Vane said as they both climbed over the railing and down into one of the longboats.

Captain Vane, Mr. England, and the crew worked throughout the day pulling up chests from the shipwrecks hull and rowing the valuables they found back to their ship.

When darkness fell, Juan, Louis, Carlos, and the others made their way close to the shore, dragging the baskets and anxious to get into the water, away from the hordes of mosquitos.

However, their success depended on getting aboard undetected and they had to wait until the crew was fall down drunk. All they could do was to bury themselves in the sand and hide from the onslaught of the blood deprived insects.

As midnight approached, Captain Vane and his pyrates were counting their spoils and drinking to their good fortune. Besides finding silver and gold, there was plenty of salvaged rum and wine now onboard their ship.

The rowdiness continued until most of the men were so drunk that they either passed out on deck or barely made it to their hammocks.

When they thought it was the right time, Carlos, Juan, Louis and the others moved their cages to the water's edge and slid them into the small waves. Inside the cages with their weapons, they grabbed the edges of the cages and started slowly kicking in the direction of the ship.

Getting away from the insects and starting to move towards the ship was a relief. It was a clear moonless night and after a few bumps from the bottom of the cage they were reminded why they went to the trouble of building them.

They were now past the half-way point and the challenge and anxiety of taking over the ship was starting to show on their faces. Still, Vane's ship was the only deliverance that could get them out of this situation and save their lives.

So far, no one on the ship had spotted them as they approached the ship. Lapping waves on the ship's hull was the only noise to be heard and they could see no one near the ladder.

They quietly moved the longboats to the side and Louis motioned his men to move closer to the ship's ladder. Louis raised his knife as a signal for all the men to cut their cages apart so they would drift away from the ship. Louis swam to the ladder and crept slowly up until he could just barely see over the railing.

Several of the crew had passed out on the deck and Louis figured that the rest must have made it to their hammocks. Louis turned around and motioned for everyone to get up on the ladder.

"Follow me and keep close together, make no sound," Louis spoke softly but sternly.

With Louis leading, they crossed over the railing and headed for the decks below. As they passed the gun deck only a few of the crew who didn't make it to their hammocks were asleep on the floor.

As they quietly stepped down the stairs to the supply deck, Louis turned around to make sure everyone was close together and then he gestured with his finger for silence.

Following Louis they made their way by the sleeping drunks, some of them in their hammocks while others were either about to fall from their hammock or had already fallen to the floor.

The snoring was intense and covered the noise from the creaking of footsteps as the men made their way to a door on the floor that led down below the supply deck.

Louis lifted the door slowly and motioned for the men to climb down. One by one they climbed down the stairs guided by the slimmest of light seeping through cracks in the deck above.

They had just entered the bowls of the ship where ballast rocks were laid and rats made their home. The men would be miserable for the next few hours sitting on rocks and fending off the creatures that lived there.

Chapter 10

"Let's go you drunken dogs, let's get our prize before the Spanish ships arrive," Mr. England shouted as the crew rolled out of their hammocks and pulled themselves off the floor.

"There's no time for grub, grab some bread and into the longboats," Captain Vane ordered. "There'll be plenty of time for feasting after we have gotten the Spanish silver."

Louis, Juan, Carlos, and the other crew members were huddling together to stay warm in the cold, dark, rat pit of the ship. Hearing the crew start to leave was a blessing and they started to prepare for the fight to come.

As soon as they thought that all the crew had left for the main deck, Louis told them to check their weapons and motioned for them to follow him up the stairs. He slowly lifted the door and finding no one about he pushed open the door and they made their way up to the gun deck.

"Mr. Langford, you have the ship," Captain Vane said as he stepped into the second longboat. "Fire a single shot for any sighting of a ship."

"Aye, Captain," Mr. Langford said.

Louis had dispersed his crew on the main deck to find out how many were left on board to guard the ship. They found that it was Mr. Langford and three of Vane's crew. Louis sent his crew back to their positions and told them to wait for his signal.

Louis waited until the longboats reached the shipwreck before he tried to take the ship. As Captain Vane approached the wreck, Louis signaled his crew to act and they took down Mr. Langford and Vane's three crew members.

"Mr. England, what is that floating in the surf?" Captain Vane shouted out after spotting part of one of the cages.

And before Mr. England could respond, Captain Vane shouted "Turn back to the ship, row you dogs, row with everything you have."

"Throw the three crewmen overboard," Louis shouted to his men. "Carlos, you and the crew set the main sail."

"Juan, cut the anchor rope," Louis ordered. "Quickly, so we can be on our way."

"Mr. Langford, what will it be, the ship's pilot or swimming with the sharks?" Louis asked as he pointed his pistol at Mr. Langford's head.

"Ship's pilot and two shares of the treasure in the Captain's quarters that was promised to me," Mr. Langford responded.

"Done," Louis replied not fully understanding what that treasure might be.

Juan took an axe from the mast hold and started cutting the anchor rope while Carlos and the crew climbed up the main mast to drop the sail.

Rifle shots rang out from the longboats but they were too far away to find a mark.

Mr. Langford took the helm and Juan took a final blow with the axe and the ship was free.

Carlos and the crew dropped the main sail and the ship started to move.

"Captain Vane, your ship will be left in the harbor at Nassau, here's two water barrels to help you get there," Louis shouted as he tossed the barrels over the side railing and the ship moved quickly away from the pursuing longboats.

"I'll track you down through hell itself if that's what it takes," Captain Vane shouted back in such a rage that Juan could feel it down to his bones.

"What heading Captain Louis?" Mr. Langford asked.

"South, along the shore," Captain Louis replied.

"So now it's Captain Louis," Juan said laughingly.

"Yes, someone has to be Captain," Louis said. "You'll be first mate and Carlos will be quartermaster."

"Aye, Captain Louis," Carlos said approaching the helm. "Now let's go pick up the ladies."

Captain Vane ordered the longboats to row out to where the ship used to be and they picked up the three pyrates and the two water barrels.

"They got the best of you, did they men?" Captain Vane asked snarling and furious about losing the ship.

"Captain, there were too many of them and only a few of us," one of the pyrates replied.

"What about Mr. Langford, is he dead?" Captain Vane asked.

"Not sure Captain, the last we saw was that Louis had a pistol to his head as they threw us over the rail," another of the pyrates replied.

"Then all is not lost, for no shot was fired on the ship," Captain Vane thought to himself.

"Mr. England, back to the wreck," Captain Vane ordered. "We need sail and rigging for both longboats."

Upon reaching the wreck, the crew collected whatever they could find to start building the rigging for both longboats. The collapsed mizzen mast was in pieces but there was enough timber to fashion the mast and boom for each boat that could hold sail even in a heavy wind.

The crew found enough rope from throughout the wreck to start putting each new rigging structure together. They started assembling the mast and boom while others found large sails inside the wreck that they could cut down to fit the new structure.

The crew worked quickly and had enough accumulated skills to assemble the new rigging for both longboats and then to cut and match the sail to the mast and boom.

After completing the assembly of the rigging, the crew found the additional rope in the wreck needed to stabilize the mast on each longboat.

There was no room for error, once out on the open ocean there would be no available resources to repair any failure to the two new sailing rigs.

"Mr. England, it looks like they may have struck a deal with Mr. Langford and I'm hoping that is what happened," Captain Vane said as they watched their crew put the new rigging up on one of the longboats.

"That scumbag Louis said they were going to the harbor at Nassau to leave the ship, what do you think?" Mr. England said.

"When they find out how much treasure is onboard our ship, they will turn," Captain Vane replied. "What's in our favor is that Mr. Langford and I have an agreement to rendezvous in case of such a situation."

"What I hope is that Mr. Langford stays true and does not turn in the face of all that treasure," Captain Vane scowled as he examined the rigging on the second longboat and told the crew to prepare to set sail in an easterly direction.

Carmen, Maria, and the other two survivors spent another wretched night on the beach covered in sand, trying to fend off the blood thirsty mosquitos. They didn't start a fire so as not to draw attention to their position and as they waited for the ship to pick them up, they all started to worry since it had not appeared by mornings light.

"Captain Louis, shipwreck ahead," Mr. Langford shouted.

"That's what we are looking for Mr. Langford," Louis replied.

"Carlos, raise the main sail and stay with Mr. Langford so the ship doesn't go a wandering," Louis said. "Juan and I will row ashore to pick up the girls and survivors."

Carmen and Maria were ecstatic to see their brother and were even more elated to climb into the longboat and get to the safety of the ship.

They all worked together to bring the longboat back onboard the ship and then everyone helped to drop the main sail to get underway.

"Carlos, have the crew to also set the top sail," Louis shouted.

"Aye, Aye, Captain," Carlos shouted back.

"Mr. Langford, can you sail us to the harbor at Nassau?" Louis asked.

"Aye, Captain," Mr. Langford replied as he turned the ship eastward toward the Bahama Channel.

"And now Mr. Langford, what of this treasure that you were promised two shares?" Louis said.

"We need to go to the Captain's quarters," Mr. Langford replied.

"Juan, we need you to take the helm," Louis shouted.

As soon as Juan approached the ship's wheel, Louis told him to keep the ship pointed directly towards the eastern horizon. Then, Louis followed Mr. Langford below as they made their way back to the Captain's quarters.

Seeing the padlock on the Captain's cabin, Louis asked where the key was.

"Only Captain Vane has the key but I took the liberty to make a duplicate in case of situations such as this," Mr. Langford said as he lifted the key from around his neck and unlocked the door.

Immediately upon entering the quarters, Louis set his eyes on the four wooden chests in the corner of the cabin and noticed that there were no locks on any of the chests. He tried to lift the lids but they would not open.

"Mr. Langford, have you seen the contents of the chests?" Louis asked.

"Only briefly, Captain Vane mainly kept it to himself," Mr. Langford replied.

"Do you know how to open the chests?" Louis asked.

"Captain Louis, will I be getting my two shares?" Mr. Langford asked.

"Of course man, now open the chests!" Louis ordered.

Mr. Langford remembered the vicinity of where the trigger lay for the first chest and began tapping each piece of wood, listening for the hollow sound as he had done for Captain Vane. When he heard it, he pushed down on the piece of wood and slid the tiny door back to reveal the trigger for the lock.

Once opened Louis walked over to the chest and stared motionless. He stood for several minutes in front of the chest, spellbound at the sight of so much exquisite jewelry and gold. He could not believe that so much wealth was standing in front of him.

"Are the others like this one?" Louis asked.

"Yes, just as splendid as the one before you," Mr. Langford replied.

"Mr. Langford, this stays between you and I," Louis ordered.

"I will tell the others that it is best to keep these cabins locked so as not to arouse further revenge from Captain Vane," Louis said as he dropped the lid shut.

"Aye Captain, I agree, the less who know the better it is for them," Mr. Langford replied.

Part III

Catt Island

Chapter 11

Two days sailing to the east was Nassau, fast becoming a haven for seamen seeking to crew on pyrate vessels. News was spreading fast about the wreck of the Spanish Armada and several pyrate sloops had already departed Nassau bound for the Florida coast.

Captain Sam Bellamy and his quartermaster Paulsgrave Williams had used their own financial assets to get started in the business and they and their pyrate crews intended to salvage the Spanish silver from the shipwrecks and then return to Nassau to divide the spoils.

"Mr. Williams, sail on the horizon," a crewman shouted from the top of the mast.

"Mr. Williams, what say you?" Captain Bellamy asked his quartermaster.

"It's a frigate flying the black flag, it looks like Vane's flag," replied Mr. Williams as he lowered his scope.

"Most unusual Mr. Williams, why would he be flying his flag at this point, he doesn't even know who we are?" Captain Bellamy responded, bewildered by the ship's action.

"Something's not right," Captain Bellamy proclaimed. "Mr. Williams, strike our flag and signal the other sloop that we'll be paying a visit to Captain Vane's ship."

"Aye, Captain," Mr. Williams replied as he signaled the other sloop to follow.

"Louis, two sails on the horizon," Juan shouted from the port bow.

"Mr. Langford, do we have a scope?" Louis asked.

"Captain Vane always kept it with him," Mr. Langford replied. "It might be below, if he left it for safe keeping."

"Juan, see if you can find a scope in one of the cabins below," Louis shouted.

Juan searched several of the cabins below but there was no sign of a scope. Reaching Captain Vane's cabin he found it padlocked and after several attempts to bust the door down, he stopped and started back up the stairs toward the helm. However, returning to inform Louis, he found there were more urgent matters at hand.

"Juan, help Carlos with the cannon," Louis said. "The two sloops are closing fast and they are flying the black flag."

A cannon shot rang out from the first approaching sloop and the shot landed close to the port side of the ship.

"Captain, they mean for us to lower our sails or there will be more to come," Mr. Langford said as he spun the ships wheel hard to starboard to avoid colliding with the sloop that was now approaching the ship's bow.

"Carlos, can we answer with the cannon?" Louis shouted.

"We are outmanned and the cannons are not ready for action, it would be suicide," Carlos shouted back.

Captain Bellamy's crew was a fierce lot, standing at the rail ready to board Vane's ship.

"Carlos, raise the main sail," Louis ordered.

Captain Bellamy had the sloop's sails lowered and ordered grappling hooks thrown onto Vane's ship. With no resistance Captain Bellamy and his men took the ship and Mr. Williams immediately recognized Mr. Langford.

"Mr. Langford, where is Captain Vane?" Mr. Williams asked.

"Captain Louis here borrowed the ship from Captain Vane who is presently a castaway on the Florida coast," Mr. Langford replied with a twitch in his eye.

"Men, search the ship," Captain Bellamy ordered.

"Captain Louis, how long have you been a Captain," Captain Bellamy asked.

"Captain, please, take what you like and we will be on our way," Louis responded ignoring his insult.

"Into the brig with all of them except for Mr. Langford," Captain Bellamy ordered.

"Captain, there are chests of silver below in the ship's hold," one of the crew shouted.

"Captain, several of the ships cabins are padlocked including the Captain's," another one of the crew shouted.

"Mr. Langford, what say you," Captain Bellamy asked as he placed a pistol to Mr. Langford's head.

"Captain, we found two Spanish shipwrecks with the first in line being wrecked beneath the waves. We dove for the chests of silver until the sharks took over and then we went back to work on the second ship which was wrecked on the beach," Mr. Langford said trembling as Captain Bellamy lowered his pistol.

"Is that where Captain Louis stole this ship from Captain Vane?" Captain Bellamy asked.

"Yes Captain, and both Captain Vane and Captain Louis promised me two shares of the treasure found in the Captain's cabin," Mr. Langford replied nervously.

"I'll wager Captain Vane was beside himself in agony over losing such a treasure as this?" Bellamy surmised.

"Dreadfully Captain, he swore revenge even if he had to go to hell and back to retrieve it," Mr. Langford replied.

"And he would definitely do just that," Bellamy said as he turned to Mr. Williams.

"Mr. Williams, please show Mr. Langford to the brig and then meet me in the Captain's cabin," Bellamy ordered.

"Captain, I have the key to Captain Vane's cabin and I know how to unlock the four chests," Mr. Langford said quickly hoping not to be taken below.

"Very well, Mr. Langford," Bellamy said.

"Mr. Williams find someone to take the helm and then join us in the Captain's quarters," Bellamy ordered as he took the arm of Mr. Langford and led him down the steps to the deck below.

Captain Bellamy and Mr. Langford made their way to Captain Vane's cabin where Mr. Langford unlocked the door and then the four chests.

Captain Bellamy saw right away that the chests were special. They were not the usual silver and gold coins that the Spanish shipped back to the King. Mr. Williams examined the gold jewels when he arrived and could not believe their good fortune in finding such a horde of exquisite valuables.

"Captain Vane will search to the ends of the earth to get back what was taken from under his nose," Captain Bellamy proclaimed as he admired a gold crucifix lined with emeralds.

"Yes Captain, Vane is not a man to be ignored," Mr. Williams replied. "If we take this ship, Vane will be hunting us for the rest of our days."

"There are too many of us now for word not to eventually get back to him and nail our coffins shut," Captain Bellamy said. "A slip of the tongue, late at night, will be all he needs to start a trail back to us."

"Captain Louis told Captain Vane that he would leave this ship for him at Nassau," Mr. Langford said.

"If we want to avoid Vane then we would have to avoid Abaco, Nassau and Port Royal," Captain Bellamy surmised.

"Mr. Williams, we need a plan to keep this to ourselves," Captain Bellamy said as he stroked his long beard.

"We keep the men that are already on the ship and who know of the treasure. You take the rest of the men to sail the two sloops to the Spanish wrecks and start salvaging, telling no one of what we have on this ship," Captain Bellamy said as he placed the gold crucifix into his coat pocket and closed the lid on the chest.

"But the men on the sloops will ask about you and this ship," Mr. Williams said.

"Tell them the truth, that these Spanish dogs stole Vane's ship and that we are going to ransom the Spaniards and then return the ship to Vane. At this point they are more interested in the shipwrecks with the Spanish silver than this ship," Captain Bellamy replied.

"What we will actually be doing is finding a safe island where we can divide the shares among this crew for the gold and silver that lies in the hole and let them disperse quietly. These four chests will be divided amongst us three, two for me and one for each of you," Captain Bellamy said.

"If the rest of the crew ever finds out about our plot then they will slit our throats only after we beg for it in lieu of the torture that they would inflict upon all of us," Mr. Williams said.

"Now is the chance for us to take our commission and escape to a life that will be better than any of this," Captain Bellamy replied.

"I'm for it," Mr. Langford said.

"Aye, your right, this is our chance, let's take it," Mr. Williams agreed.

"Mr. Williams and Mr. Langford, make your mark on the chest you want and rest assured that we will find an island and bury these four chests to be retrieved when all three of us return together," Captain Bellamy said as they clasped hands in agreement.

Chapter 12

"Drop the sail and signal Mr. England to do the same," Captain Vane ordered as they approached the Nassau harbor and the two longboats pulled alongside one another.

"Mr. England, they would spot me right off, take some men into town and see if there is any sign of our ship. If not, then learn of how we might obtain a ship worth sailing," Captain Vane ordered.

"Aye Captain," Mr. England replied.

"We will wait for you here and be mindful not to disclose our reasons," Captain Vane shouted as the longboat pulled away.

Vane did not expect his ship to be in the harbor and he knew that they would probably have to take one, possibly by using force, which he would leave for his crew to deal with.

Mr. England and his crew reached the shore outside the town and beached the longboat. Taking three men with him into town, he ordered the rest to stay and guard the longboat.

As they passed the docks, Mr. England did not see their ship but he did notice a fine sloop at the end of the docks.

The town was growing fast with new pubs and brothels going up along the main street to feed the throngs of cutthroats and ladies flocking to the frenzy for Spanish silver.

Blending in with the crowds of seaman roaming the cobbled streets, they searched for the right tavern and chose one with the largest gathering of rogues to enter and order rum.

"Wench, rum all around, and be quick for our throats are dry," Mr. England shouted to a pretty young girl who was serving the unruly crowd of thieves and scoundrels.

The young girl returned with a jug of rum and as she poured, she asked if they wanted any of the pig roasting on the fire.

"Perhaps later, and what be your name?" Mr. England asked the girl.

"My name is Jane and that will be one silver for the rum," Jane said.

"Jane, please sit for a moment, we noticed a sloop that is moored at the end of the docks and would like to know who we should speak with about signing on," Mr. England said as he placed two silvers in front of her.

"They brought her in last week and they say that she is filled with stockings and lace hats from France," Jane said as she took the two silvers and placed them for safe keeping.

"And who be they?" Mr. England asked placing two more silvers in front of her.

"Why, Captain Hornigold of course, but he sailed yesterday for the Spanish wrecks," Jane said as she happily took the two silvers and placed them with the other two.

"Jane, we were wondering if you might be able to take some rum to the crew of the sloop to help make their task easier and to learn of the ships attributes?" Mr. England asked as he laid two gold coins in front of her.

"Two gold now and two when you return with all the particulars," Mr. England offered.

"Three gold now and three when I return," Jane counter offered with an engaging smile.

"Done," Mr. England replied as he laid down one more gold coin.

Jane had already guessed what they must be up to and since Captain Hornigold and his quartermaster, Mr. Teach, had gone a wrecking, she figured that it was only fair for her to earn some gold and have a good time too.

"Hey Roberts, look what's sashaying down the walkway and carrying what looks to be two jugs of rum," seaman Billings said as he was standing watch on the deck of Captain Hornigold's newly acquired sloop.

"Mr. Billings, permission to come aboard your ship with compliments from the establishment?" Jane asked in her most suggestive manner.

"Mr. Billings, Captain Hornigold won't like this, it'll be our heads if something goes wrong," Roberts warned Mr. Billings.

"Captain Hornigold and Mr. Teach are off a wrecking and nothing will happen if you keep your mouth shut," Mr. Billings told Roberts.

"Jane, please come aboard and watch your step on the first plank, it's a bit unsteady," Mr. Billings said as he reached out his hand to help.

Mr. England had ordered another round for his crew as Jane entered the tavern through the rear door. She got them a full jug of rum and took a seat next to Mr. England.

"You took your own sweet time, missy," Mr. England snarled. "My crew is nearly all drunk."

"Sometimes the particulars don't come as easy as you might expect," Jane said snarling back.

"And what be those particulars?" Mr. England asked.

"Did you already forget about my five gold?" Jane asked.

"No missy, and it's still three gold as we agreed," Mr. England replied as he placed the three gold coins next to the jug of rum on the table.

"Mr. Billings says she is a fine sailing sloop, fast on the breakaway, with new French rifles still in the box. There are four pyrates including Mr. Billings and they are all drunk and probably passing out now as we speak," Jane said.

"Thanks missy, I wish I could stay longer," Mr. England said as he gestured to the crew to finish their rum.

"Sir, I want to return to Port Royal, this place isn't living up to its expectations. Can you help me?" Jane asked with an enticing smile.

"If at any other time, I would gladly accommodate your request," Mr. England replied as he rose and summoned his crew to follow.

Mr. England and his men returned to the site of the longboat and woke the rest of the crew to tell them of the sloop and how it was barely crewed.

As they approached the ship in their longboat there was no sign of movement so they quickly boarded the sloop, subdued the drunken crew, and tied them to the dock.

Then they quietly lifted the ropes, raised the main sail, and slowly sailed away from the dock.

Drawing close to their rendezvous point, Mr. England used a lantern to signal Captain Vane and his crew to come aboard the sloop.

"Mr. England, any sign of our ship?" Vane asked as he climbed over the rail and onto the deck.

"None Captain, so we took this sloop to help find it," Mr. England replied as he took the helm.

"Well done Mr. England, this looks like a fine sloop to get us back our ship," Captain Vane said as he looked her over.

"Men, to your stations, let's make her fly and get back what was taken from us," Captain Vane shouted to the crew.

"Mr. England, set a course east to Eleuthera, then south to Catt Island," Captain Vane ordered. "If our luck holds, then we'll be meeting up with Mr. Langford in no time soon."

Chapter 13

"Mr. Langford, the rollers are building," Captain Bellamy said as he watched the waves grow larger.

"Aye Captain, it's a large blow coming from the southeast," Mr. Langford replied.

"Let me take the helm, tell Pete to feed the crew before the storm takes hold and to use only fresh meat," Bellamy ordered.

"They'll be plenty busy when the storm breaks," Bellamy thought as he turned the wheel to face the oncoming waves.

Mr. Langford made his way to the galley and passed the word to the cook, "one arm Pete."

During a storm, while sailing with Captain Hornigold, Pete got his hand caught between the mast and jib leaving it mashed and useless. Gangrene set in and soon his whole arm was gone. Captain Hornigold was the only one who wanted to save his place among the crew and cooking was what he was able to do.

"What does he expect? All we have is some meat that's ready to turn and a few onions. It'll be meat soup and they had better like it," Pete said as he started throwing everything into a pot.

"The waves are starting to get bigger and I'm starting to get seasick," Maria said as she moved closer to the corner of their cell.

"I remember when I once thought the rolling waves were beautiful and now I know that they are only a curse on what's to follow," Carmen moaned and lowered her head onto her knees.

"We should have had the cannons ready just in case something like this happened. Then we might not be in this predicament," Carlos said as he looked earnestly at Louis.

"Be quiet someone's coming," Louis said sternly in a low voice.

"Okay Spaniards, you're in luck, there's plenty of soup and bread," Pete said as he put down a half bucket of soup and some bread in front of their cell and went back up the stairs.

"I'm starving, let me at it," Carlos said as he moved to the cell door and lifted a cup of the soup from the bucket.

"You better let Carmen check it or you might be sorry you drank it," Juan warned as Carlos took a long drink from the mug.

Carlos choked and spit out what he could of the soup. Carmen grabbed the mug and dipped it into the bucket. Smelling and then taking a small finger taste Carmen confirmed that the soup was foul and it would take only a little bit to turn a bull into a cow.

"This crew is destined to be out of operation in only a matter of hours," Louis said as he rested his back on the cell bars. "If we could only open the cell door then we could probably take the ship back."

On deck, after only an hour the crew was starting to drop like flies. Many ran for the poop deck but most did not make it more than ten steps before heaving their guts out all over the deck. Then came the real need for the poop deck and many could not find a place in the crowd, leaving them to let their bowls flow freely on the deck as well.

"Push with all you're might, back and forth and again," Louis said as they all tried to loosen the bars that were embedded in the wooden floor. Hearing steps coming down the stairs, they all quit pushing the bars and sat back down on the floor.

"Captain Louis, I see that all of you except for one stayed away from the soup," Mr. Langford said as he made his way to their cell.

"Yes, we're lucky we had extra buckets for Carlos," Louis said looking over at Carlos who was lying on the cell floor in agony. "Is this you're doing, Mr. Langford?"

"Not exactly, I just happened to see what was going into the cooking pot and decided to forget about eating," Mr. Langford said sitting down next to the bucket of soup.

"This ship is ours again, that is, if you and I can make an agreement about the four chests in Captain Vane's cabin," Mr. Langford said dangling the key to the cell in front of his face.

"We split fifty-fifty, two chests for me and two chests for you and the rest of your crew," Mr. Langford said. "Do we have an agreement?"

"What chests?" Juan and Carmen both asked chiming in at the same time.

"I'll tell you later," Louis said.

"Agreed, Mr. Langford, now get us out of here," Louis ordered as Mr. Langford turned the key and opened the cell door.

"The whole crew and Captain Bellamy are flat on the deck in agony just like young Carlos there. There's one longboat left that we can make them climb into and then set them adrift," Mr. Langford said as they started up towards the main deck.

The main deck was littered with the crew all lying in the horizontal position, clutching their stomachs and moaning obscenities, most of them directed towards Pete who was also flat on his back.

Louis, Juan, and Mr. Langford tied up Captain Bellamy, placed him in the longboat, and then lowered it over the starboard side while Carmen, Maria, and the other survivors and crewmen collected all the weapons on the main deck.

They then started either picking up the pyrates or dragging them to the starboard rail. A few of the pyrates didn't like the idea of going into the longboat in the rolling seas but quickly relented when they saw that Captain Bellamy was tied up and a pistol was pointed to their head.

Louis let go the rope tied to the longboat and a few of the pyrates who still retained some sort of reasoning lifted their finger in defiance and shouted oaths of vengeance.

There were three dead pyrates, including Pete, left on the main deck. Juan and the other two survivors dragged their bodies to the starboard rail and started to throw them overboard.

"Isn't someone going to say anything for them?" Carmen asked stepping closer to the dead men.

Mr. Langford stepped forward and taking off his hat he bowed his head. "Lord, these men were sons of England and they were only doing what was right by them. They are now in your hands, may they rest in peace."

With that, their bodies were thrown overboard.

"Juan, would you see if Carlos is still alive and if he is, help him up to the main deck," Louis said.

"Carmen and Maria throw everything overboard that had to do with cooking that stew. We don't want to lose anyone else," Louis said.

"Mr. Langford, can we outrun the storm?" Louis asked.

"She's coming from the southeast, the only way to outrun her will be to head northeast so we can attempt to miss her fury," Mr. Langford replied as he took the helm.

"That would give us a heading towards Catt Island," Louis worriedly surmised.

"It's heading northeast or possibly sinking the ship while fighting the storm," Mr. Langford replied.

"Northeast it is, Mr. Langford," Louis replied.

"Aye, Aye Captain," Mr. Langford replied.

The waves were continuing to build and as Mr. Langford turned the rudder, several of the larger waves washed over the bow and cleared the main deck of the putrid remains. He caught a glimpse of the longboat heading north away from the storm and he knew that Captain Bellamy and his pyrates might have a chance of reaching an island, if they recuperated and started rowing.

Chapter 14

"Mr. England, I think it would be wise to have cannon on board," Captain Vane shouted over the steady southeast wind as he stood at the railing of the newly acquired sloop.

"Agreed, there's no telling what we will run into when we try to get back our ship," Mr. England shouted as he turned the ships wheel to compensate for the southeasterly wind.

"We're headed for Eleuthera, let's quietly check Harbour Island to see what may be anchored there," Captain Vane ordered.

"Aye Captain, Harbour Island it is," Mr. England replied.

Pyrate's Sanctuary

The islands surrounding Nassau were fast becoming a pyrate's refuge. Abaco Island to the north, Eleuthera Island to the east and Catt Island to the Southeast became hiding places for the pyrate's acquisitions. Harbour Island was small and located just two miles east of the larger Eleuthera Island. Pyrates used Eleuthera Island for whatever was convenient but the English and Spanish warships would use Harbour Island for staging ambushes on pyrate ships. Both England and Spain had suffered losses to the growing number of pyrates and wanted them eliminated. [10,11]

"Lights, lights near the island," Mr. England shouted out.

"What direction, Mr. England?" Captain Vane asked as he made his way towards the helm.

"Off the port bow, Captain," Mr. England replied.

"Aye, two sets, one must be the ship at anchor and the other a campfire from the island," Vane surmised.

"Drop anchor here and send out the longboat to take a look at the ship," Vane ordered.

The longboat was lowered and six men rowed it to within one hundred yards of the anchored ship. Captain Vane was surprised at how quickly they returned.

"It's an English war frigate with at least thirty to forty cannon, it looks like almost all the crew are ashore," said one of the pyrates as he climbed up the port ladder.

"We thought they might have seen us, so we rowed like never before but no shots were fired," another one of the pyrates said.

"Men, this is our chance, if we strike now we can have a ship of the line to help retrieve our silver and gold," Vane told his crew.

"We need a diversion to keep the English soldiers away from the ship so we can capture and sail her away from her current owners," Vane proposed.

"Mr. England, what if you and five other brave lads were to go ashore and secure yourselves behind the encampment. Then, when ready, open fire and wound or kill as many soldiers as possible. That would draw all the attention to your location," Vane suggested.

"What say ye men, who will join me to go ashore?" Mr. England shouted out.

No one moved forward or offered to put their life on the line. Silence was all that was heard.

"Each man that goes ashore will receive an extra share of the silver and gold that was stolen from us," Vane offered as hands flew into the air.

Mr. England stepped forward and selected the pyrate's that he wanted to join him.

"Mr. England, each man will take two rifles and two pistols. When you are ready, empty your weapons into the English soldiers and then run for the southern tip of the island. We will get into position and wait for your first volley of lead," Captain Vane said as Mr. England and the five pyrates loaded the launch with their weapons.

Vane knew that surprise makes all the difference, so when his sloop was within two hundred yards of the English frigate he had nine of his crew to quietly row the longboat within striking distance of the frigate.

When the first volley of lead was heard coming from the shore line, Captain Vane advanced his sloop toward the frigate.

When the English soldiers on the ship spotted the sloop coming toward them they let go a volley of lead towards Captain Vane's sloop.

The pyrates in the longboat had managed to draw alongside the frigate without being detected and when the English soldiers fired their weapons the pyrates raced up the ships ladder and overwhelmed the soldiers.

The pyrates gave no quarter and finished off all of the English soldiers as Captain Vane's sloop moved alongside the frigate. Captain Vane then ordered most of his crew onto the frigate and joined them on the new acquisition.

"Move lively men, cut the anchor line, throw the dead English soldiers over the rail, and set the main sail. Quickly men, before those on shore reach our new ship and ask for its return," Captain Vane ordered laughing as he watched the soldiers scrambling to move their longboats off the beach and into the surf.

On shore Mr. England and the pyrates had emptied their weapons into the English soldiers and then took off running for the southern tip of the island.

The soldiers started to pursue the pyrates but then they heard the rifle shots coming from the ship. Confused, they figured it must be a trick and their first priority was to defend the ship.

They rushed back to their longboats and tried to make their way through the surf but their actions were futile as the frigate and the sloop quietly sailed away.

In short order, the sloop sailed in close to shore at the southern point of the island and picked up Mr. England and the other pyrates.

"Good work Mr. England, was anyone hit in the skirmish?" Captain Vane asked as he helped him aboard the English frigate.

"Many of the soldiers dropped where they stood. As for us, we outran the remaining soldier's bullets as if our tails were on fire," Mr. England said laughing as he stepped onto the newly acquired frigate.

By morning both ships were sailing southward towards Catt Island. The wind was increasing out of the southeast and the ships were tacking back and forth to make headway.

"There must be a big blow coming with such waves," Vane thought to himself as he watched the waves growing larger with each set.

Chapter 15

"Captain Louis, the weather, she's getting worse," Mr Langford shouted out over the howling wind.

"Juan tell the crew to start securing the gear for heavy weather and lock down the hatches," Louis ordered as he braced himself for a large wave just about to hit the stern.

"Mr. Langford, can we outrun the storm?" Louis asked as he tied a safety rope to the ships wheel.

"If our luck is still with us, then we have a fair chance of beating it," Mr. Langford said, hoping that his luck had not yet run out.

The crew had rigged for full sail and brought out the foresail to speed the ship away from the approaching southeast storm. But even with the strong wind at their back and full sail the waves were growing larger and began crashing down on the stern of the ship.

Juan made sure Carmen and Maria were safe in a cabin below and Carlos joined Mr. Langford to help keep the helm steady. It took two men to keep the rudder stable under the enormous force when sliding down a wave. With each slide the crew had to scramble to find a hold and brace themselves for the impact at the bottom.

It was a long night, made worse by not being able to see the huge waves that fell relentlessly onto the deck. The ship was able to stay just ahead of the storm during the night and by morning the waves were diminishing.

Luck was still with them, the ship was intact and the crew had suffered no injuries. The only problem now was finding out where the storm had placed the ship.

"Mr. Langford, what's your best guess?" Louis asked as he lowered the scope belonging to Captain Vane.

"Captain Louis, we traveled a great distance to the east. My guess is that we are either on one side or the other of Long Island," Mr. Langford speculated.

"Louis, we all want to know about the four chests in Captain Vane's cabin," Juan said as he and the girls approached the helm.

"Mr. Langford, let's head west to see if we end up at Long Island and I'll be needing the key temporarily," Louis ordered as he accepted the key to Vane's cabin.

"You have the helm, I have matters to discuss below," Louis said as he stepped down the stairs to the main deck with Juan and the girls following.

"Carlos, will you join us below in the Captain's cabin," Louis shouted to Carlos who was just starting to help set the main sail.

Carlos made his way to the Captain's cabin and entered just as Louis unlocked the last of the four chests. Juan, Carmen, Maria, and Carlos stared at the wealth before them and then they all collapsed into the chairs surrounding Vane's supper table.

"We're dead, all of us, we are dead," Carlos said as he held his head in his hands.

"There are many more chests of silver in the ships hold that Vane and his crew salvaged from the Capitana," Louis said as he picked up one of the gold pieces and then sat down in the chair at Vane's desk.

"Vane will make us all pray for death as he rips out our organs and feeds them one by one to his bloodthirsty crew," Carlos moaned as if a knife had been thrust into his gut.

"We do as we intended, take the ship and its treasure to Nassau and leave it for Vane to pick up," Juan said hoping for a simple solution.

"We would have to stay with the ship so that no one else would steal it and when Vane arrives he will kill us all," Louis said as he held and admired a small bird cage made out of gold.

"Not only did we steal his ship but also a king's treasure with which he could sail to England and retire from pyrating altogether," Carlos added as he walked over to a chest and picked up a gold box lined with emeralds.

"Then we need to melt the gold and silver so it is unrecognizable, then divide it amongst ourselves and find another ship," Juan proposed as he too walked over to the chests and stared blindly at the wealth.

"Juan, let's forget all of this, we still have our fathers gold buried at the wreck. Let's make our way back to it and then find a way to Seville," Carmen argued.

"Sisters, we could easily die from the hands of other pyrates or natives trying to recover our fathers gold. Even though Vane is probably hunting us, this wealth is in our hands right now and we must not lose this opportunity to help us get back to our family," Juan said as he tried to convince the girls to help them.

"There's nothing else we could do other than die at the hands of Vane and his crew," Louis joined in agreement.

"I'm with you, let's make an accord and move quickly to find a place to melt it all," Carlos said as he tossed the box back into the pile of gold.

"Captain Bellamy, a ship," Mr. Noland said pointing to a spot on the northern horizon.

They had been adrift in the longboat for days after being cast away from Vane's ship and Mr. Noland, Bellamy's quartermaster, had just sighted their salvation.

"Men, keep a sharp out for any cannons and the flag she's flying," Bellamy shouted to the crew.

They had only just barely missed the wrath of the storm by being driven to the west as the storm moved to the north. They had finished the water that was stowed away in the longboat and were now hoping that the approaching ship was a merchant.

"Mr. Noland, whether it be a merchant or a war ship we will say that pyrates thieved our merchant and set us adrift in this longboat," Bellamy said as he took off his sash that once held his pistols.

"Men, lose any evidence of having had weaponry so they don't think us pyrates," Bellamy ordered and added "once on the ship get as close to the men with pistols and rifles as possible and wait for my signal."

"Captain, the sloop has eight starboard cannons and she is flying the French flag," shouted one of the crew from the bow of the longboat.

"Men, raise and wave your oars for rescue and get ready, we may be in for a scrap," Bellamy shouted to the crew.

The ship caught sight of the longboat and turned towards them. As the ship approached the longboat, several rifles were seen resting on the ship's starboard rail.

"Ahoy the longboat, what say you?" the Captain said with a French accent.

"Captain La Buse, it's me, Mr. Noland. I crewed under Captain Hornigold," Mr, Norland shouted to the French Captain.

"Captain La Buse, I am Captain Bellamy, permission for Mr. Norland and I to come aboard?" Bellamy shouted up to Captain La Buse.

"Permission granted, come aboard Captain," La Buse shouted back.

Captain Oliver La Buse had commanded the French sloop during the war and when it was time to return to France in 1714, La Buse and his crew turned pyrate and stayed in the Bahama Islands.

"Captain La Buse, we met with some unfortunate circumstances and lost our ship to a few rouge pirates. We would like to have your help in trying to get her back," Captain Bellamy said.

"I sympathize with your plight, but there must be particulars discussed and terms agreed upon," La Buse replied.

"Captain, time is of the upmost importance in this matter, as we speak opportunity is slowly sailing away," Bellamy intensely replied.

"Captain, you and I could have any ship we want by simply taking it, what is so important about this ship?" La Buse inquired.

"Captain La Buse, might we get rum and food for my crew first and then, you and I have a word together in your cabin?" Bellamy asked La Buse.

"Of course Captain," La Buse said as he motioned Bellamy's crew to come aboard.

"Men, help our brothers aboard and find rum and food for them all," La Buse ordered his crew.

Down below in La Buse's cabin, Bellamy shared with him the story of taking over Vane's stolen ship and then losing it. Bellamy told La Buse of the great wealth that Vane had found at the wreck of the Capitana and which now rested in the hull of Vane's ship.

"That is where we just came from," La Buse said as he poured more rum for both of them and shook his head in disbelief.

"We were near Captain Hornigold and Mr. Teach, who also had their crews diving on the wrecks, when we saw several approaching Spanish war ships," La Buse said as he settled back in his chair.

"Did you fight?" Bellamy asked as he raised his rum to drink.

"No, we saw that we were outgunned and decided to not risk losing our ship," La Buse said as a cat jumped into his lap and he stroked its head.

"What happened to Hornigold and Teach?" Bellamy asked as he put his drink down.

"Not sure, they were still diving for silver as we sailed away," La Buse said as he leaned forward in his chair and the cat jumped onto the floor.

"In what direction was the ship heading?" La Buse asked in an inquisitive manner.

"There's more," Bellamy said, being cautious not to say too much.

"Vanes's pilot is at the helm. He was there when we took the ship and the wreck survivors did not force him into the longboat with the rest of us," Bellamy said.

"Mr. Langford?" La Buse asked as if he knew him.

"Yes, the miserable dog. I fear he was responsible for putting the sickness on my crew," Bellamy said in disgust as he slammed his mug down on the Captain's table.

"From where do you know Mr. Langford," Bellamy asked.

"Mr. Langford was Captain Jennings pilot until he joined Captain Vane's crew. He's a very cunning fellow," La Buse said as he leaned back in his chair.

"Captain, do we join together to find the ship?" Bellamy asked before divulging any more information.

"The split will be sixty/forty since it's my ship," La Buse said.

"Fifty/fifty and we'll find another ship for me and my crew," Bellamy counter offered.

"Yes, we'll need another ship with more cannons to fend off Vane's revenge," La Buse speculated as they lifted their mugs in agreement.

Chapter 16

Now aboard a thirty-four cannon frigate, liberated from the English Navy, Captain Vane was still in hopes that Mr. Langford was going to hold true to their accord and reunite at Catt Island.

"Land off the port bow," a crewman cried out from atop the main mast.

"Mr. England, order the crew to keep an eye peeled for any advancing ship," Captain Vane ordered his quartermaster. Captain Vane's frigate and sloop had reached Catt Island without any sign of Vane's stolen ship. They would wait. Vane was determined to not let anything stand in the way of him and the wealth that was in the Captain's cabin and the hull of his ship.

The next day there still was no sighting of a ship so Vane had the crew to place eight of the frigate's thirty-four cannons on the sloop to make it fit for battle.

The pyrates spent three more days anchored and waiting at Devils Point with no sign of a ship. By now, the crews were becoming restless and wanted to go ashore to find fresh food on the uninhabited island.

"Mr. England, let half the crew from each ship go ashore for the day, but they must return before nightfall. I don't want any surprises and we must be prepared to act quickly," Vane told Mr. England.

The newly acquired English frigate was amply supplied with rum and the pyrates took more than enough for their time on the island. They found fresh fruit and managed to get thoroughly wasted on the rum. Not to be out done by the pyrates onshore, the rest of the crew on the two ships started drinking heavily also. By nightfall no one except Vane, England, and their pilot Mr. Yeates were able to stand much less able to fire a cannon at an approaching ship.

Ever since his ship was stolen, Vane could only get a few hours of sleep before being awakened by the same recurring night mare. In the dream he was about to be married to his childhood sweetheart when an English officer and his men took the young lady away and tossed her in jail. Vane paid a solicitor to plead for her life but because she had relations with a known pyrate, she was sentenced to hang on the gallows. As the gallows door opened beneath her feet and she dropped to her death, she looked into Vane's eyes and spoke "you will never know me". Vane always awoke, sobbing like a baby, clutching his pistol and then swearing death to the ones who killed his sweetheart.

"Captain, a ship," Mr. England yelled as he burst into the cabin and awoke Vane from his dream.

"Mr. England, what the damnation is going on?" Vane yelled back as he sat up from his bed and drew his pistol.

"Captain, a ship off the starboard side," Mr. England said as he ducked the aim of Vane's pistol.

It was early morning and the sun had not yet risen. As Vane and England stood on the ship's deck, light was faintly emerging and the silhouette of the anchored ship could barely be seen against the horizon. It was about a mile from their two ships but Vane could tell it was larger than their frigate.

"It must have arrived late in the evening and anchored for the night, not detecting us so far," Vane said to England as they peered intensely at the ship.

Not hesitating, Vane declared "we need to attack it now before her crew brings her cannons to life."

"Mr. England, go onboard the sloop and awake the crew. Cut your anchor, set the sails and make sure the cannons are loaded properly. I will do the same on this ship. In unison, you take the port side of the anchored ship and I'll take the starboard side. Then, we'll blast them back from whence they came," Vane ordered.

Both of Vane's ships quietly came to life after the crews realized that battle was imminent and their courage would soon be tested. Each ship cut their anchors, set their sails, and slowly turned towards their target.

Vane's frigate now had twenty-six cannons and Mr. England's sloop had eight cannons ready to bring forth hell fire and damnation to the sleeping intruder.

The sea was calm with just enough wind to fill the sails. The sun was close to breaking the horizon as the two ships made their way towards their mark.

Onboard the anchored ship, "Steady men, no movement," the English Captain calmly ordered his officers.

The English Captain's guess that this was their stolen frigate from Harbour Island had paid off. The rat had taken the bait and was fixing to reap the reward from the English sixty-four cannon heavy frigate in her Majesty's service.

The English Captain had planned to rendezvous with the English frigate at Harbor Island for tactical maneuvers designed to track down and capture pyrates. Upon arrival at the island the English Captain was expecting to see the frigate anchored in the harbor but instead saw no ship and only English officers, sailors and soldiers waving to them for rescue.

The English officer's, embarrassed but grateful, explained the trick that had been delivered upon them and the deaths of their comrades at the hands of the bloody pyrates. The officers wanted revenge and asked the English Captain of the heavy frigate if they could join in the pursuit of the scoundrels.

Vane's ships were now reaching the bow of the heavy frigate and could now discern that the ship was English and loaded with cannon. Vane detected no movement on the ship and he thought that they had completely taken the English crew by surprise.

As Vane's frigate and Mr. England's sloop passed the bow on each side of the heavy frigate, the English ship came alive with a thunderous roar of cannon fire.

Both Vane's and England's ships started taking hits from the twelve pound cannon balls that were rifling towards them. Vane and England opened fire with their cannons but they were not inflicting near the damage that they were receiving from the English heavy frigate.

Vane and England cursed simultaneously at their predicament and broke off the engagement only after receiving devastating blows to their ships.

Vane's frigate was mortally damaged but was able to sail beyond the range of the English cannons before she started to seriously take on water.

"Cut the anchor and drop the sails. Helm, hard to port," ordered the Captain on the English ship.

Mr. England's sloop was still seaworthy and caught up to Vane's sinking ship. Vane and what was left of his crew jumped into the sea and swam to Mr. England's sloop.

The English ship began slowly to make its turn in pursuit of Vane and England as Vane's ship slipped beneath the waves. Mr. England's sloop was faster than the heavy frigate and soon the English frigate was left behind, struggling to make any kind of headway.

1715

Part IV

Hispaniola

Chapter 17

They had sailed westward until they found Long Island where Mr. Langford had proposed sailing north to the safety of Catt Island. Louis and Carlos were suspicious of Mr. Langford's northerly interest and chose to sail south to find a suitable place to reconfigure the stamped silver coins and gold bars. They headed southeast until they saw a speck of land that Louis recognized as Crooked Island.

At the northwestern point of the island they headed south, following the shore, looking for a place where they could conceal the ship while they labored to melt the gold and silver. Around the southern tip of the island they found a large lagoon where they could anchor the ship and it would only be a short distance to the beach. Having given Bellamy and his crew their last longboat, they decided to construct a raft to haul all of the gold and silver to shore.

Without delay, the work began on building the raft using the ship's planking from the supply deck. Empty food and water barrels were lashed to the raft to help float the heavy cargo. As much rope as possible was gathered from throughout the ship and tied together so it could help pull the raft from the ship to the shore and then retrieve it back to the ship.

When construction was complete they hoisted the raft over the ship's railing with the barrels facing outwards and lowered it slowly to the waterline. Using oars they pushed the raft out away from the ship as it landed upright and floated on the barrels. Loading the raft was a balancing act, trying to get the chests of silver just right, so as not to tip the raft one way or the other.

Three of Louis's crew swam through the shark infested water and light surf to carry the rope and then pull the raft on its maiden voyage to shore. On the next trip, drinking water and the rest of the food were brought ashore to prepare for the coming night.

They started two fires close to the lagoon shore and then build several shelters out of small tree limbs and palm leaves that were about six inches off the jungle floor.

The survivors and crew hoped that mosquitos were not going to be a problem, as it was on the Florida coast, but that was the reason for two fires to help battle the intruders. Having the shelters close to the fires allowed the smoke to reduce the flying insects and provide protection against snakes and scorpions that were more than likely on the island.

Their first night proved to be much better than what they had experienced on the shores of Florida. Sleeping above ground with minimal insect attacks allowed the survivors and crew to finally sleep through the night.

The next day they found the island to be a tropical oasis with clear blue green water, tall coconut palms, and white sandy beaches stretching for miles. Fish and lobster abounded throughout the coral reefs and water was found only several miles to the north of the lagoon.

But even with all the surrounding beauty it didn't take the survivors and crew long to get into a routine that left some of the members disappointed with their position.

"Juan, we need more firewood and hurry before the pot starts to cool off," Carmen shouted as she and Maria slowly tipped the pot over so that only a fraction of the hot metal liquid poured out into a hole where it quickly cooled into a bar of silver.

"They think that because we are women we should be doing most of the melting while they go off exploring the island and getting drunk," Carmen said as they tipped the pot again to pour another bar of silver.

"So, since we are doing most of the work, every tenth bar of gold or silver will go into our hiding place so we can be rightfully compensated," Carmen said as she placed another bar of silver to the side of the pile.

"Why is this bar of silver still lying here separate from the pile?" asked Juan as he dumped the wood in his arms onto the ground near the melting pot.

"Brother, we let it cool off before we place it on the pile," Carmen replied with a smile.

"What did you and the other men find today besides more rum in the ships storage? Something to eat I hope?" asked Carmen as she and Maria started to pour another bar of silver.

"Louis and Carlos headed north along the lagoon shore to see what was on the other side of the island and Mr. Langford is on the ship directing the offloading," Juan said as he placed more wood on the fire.

"I'm going hunting for food and the others are building a better shelter and helping Mr. Langford," Juan said grabbing his knife and rifle.

"What you actually mean to say is that they are placing a few more branches on the A-frame and drinking in excess while doing it," Carmen angrily replied.

"Keep the fire hot," Juan shouted as he walked out of sight.

"These idiots are going to get us all killed," Carmen said to Maria who sat down exhausted from working in the heat.

"Let's make it every eighth bar instead of every tenth bar," Carmen said smiling at Maria as she took two bars off the pile and placed them with their other bar of silver.

As the day passed, Carmen and Maria were close to having melted all the silver at the camp and none of the crew had brought any more.

"That's strange, we haven't seen any of the men for most of the day and there is still a lot of gold and silver on the ship to be brought ashore," Carmen said to Maria as she looked around the camp.

"Hello the camp," Carlos shouted as he approached Carmen and Maria.

"Where's Louis, Juan said he went with you?" Carmen asked.

"We had planned to go together but then he decided to stay and help Mr. Langford," Carlos said as he put down several lobster that he had just caught inside the reef.

"Carmen, Maria, come quick!" Juan shouted from the beach.

Carmen, Maria, and Carlos ran from the camp and onto the beach to where Juan was looking out to sea.

"Is that our ship?" Juan asked in disbelief as he stared at the ship sailing eastward away from the island.

"It looks the very same," Carlos said also staring at the ship as the last of the sails were dropped into place.

"Carlos, where is Louis?" Juan asked hastily.

"He said he was going to help Mr. Langford offload the gold and silver," Carlos replied.

They all looked at each other and in unison they turned and started running towards the lagoon. The raft was floating empty in the lagoon with no ship in sight.

Chapter 18

"Captain Louis, don't worry, they have four chests of the silver to divide amongst themselves," Mr. Langford said noticing that Louis seemed a bit troubled at the events haven taken place.

"It's not that Mr. Langford, its Vane's vengeance. We could not have stayed there any longer and by our leave, the children are out of harm's way," Louis said as he scanned the horizon.

"The question is now, in what direction is Vane headed and what direction should we go?" Louis thought out loud as he placed his scope in his coat pocket and leaned on the ships rail.

"I always thought Catt Island was a good place to hide this bounty. It's out of the way and a quiet place where we wouldn't be disturbed in placing it where it couldn't be found," Mr. Langford said as he kept the wheel steady at the helm.

"Vane is surely on our trail. He has probably made it to Nassau and will likely go to Port Royal, where he thinks we might be heading," Louis said ignoring Mr. Langford's insistence on Catt Island.

"Then where is it going to be safe to divide our loot and go our separate ways?" Mr. Langford asked being careful not to propose another destination.

"We'll hope that Vane goes to Port Royal and we'll head southeast to the Leeward Islands. We should be able to find a

Governor there who can be persuaded to look the other way," Louis said confidently.

"Aye Captain, the Leeward Islands," Mr. Langford agreed and shouted out to the crew to adjust the sails as they turned the ship towards the southeast.

The five crew members and two survivors were loyal to Louis, so Mr. Langford was careful not to create any animosity and to keep his emotions in check.

Mr. Langford suspected that Vane was surely going to kill him now for not reaching Catt Island as agreed, regardless of what reason he gave to Vane.

"Vane probably figured he had turned for the gold and silver and there was no way now of convincing him otherwise," Mr. Langford thought to himself as he turned the rudder to fill the main sail.

"Mr. Langford, with only nine of us we will need a plan for the cannon in case we end up in a scrap," Louis said as he eyed the cannons that were positioned before him.

Vane had stolen his prize from the Spanish when this ship had failed to rendezvous with a fleet sailing to Vera Cruz and was subsequently open to attack by any passing marauder. The ship was fast for its size and carried twenty-eight cannon, fourteen cannon to starboard and fourteen to port.

"We will make sure all of the cannons are ready for action but after the first engagement, we will probably only be able to reload fourteen of them on the starboard side in time for another attack," Mr. Langford predicted.

"The odds are against us if Vane and his pyrates catch up to us. It will not be a pretty site nor a pleasant one for any of us," Mr. Langford added as he motioned to one of the crew to take in the slack on the main sail.

"I understand Mr. Langford, if you will see to the crew and readying the cannon then I will take the helm," Louis ordered as he stepped in to take over the wheel from Mr. Langford.

Mr. Langford examined all twenty-eight cannons for any sign of cracks in the iron or the carriages. When outnumbered, the nine foot 12-pounder cannons could land devastating blows against an adversary by loading it with projectiles intended to disable the pursuers. Round shot was good for hull penetration but not to cut rigging lines, make large holes in the sails, or dismember and kill the attackers. [17]

Mr. Langford had the crew to bring up double the supply of double heads, chain, and hammer shot to both the starboard and port deck cannons to be used against the pyrates and their ships rigging. Round shot was loaded in a few of the cannons in the hopes of blasting a gap in the hull of their ship. The crew practiced firing and reloading as quick as possible in anticipation of fending off the pyrates and protecting their valuable cargo.

"Captain, there she is, off the port bow," Mr. Yeates said as he turned the ships wheel to fill the main sail.

"I see her Mr. Yeates. I'll take the helm, go wake Mr. England from his beauty sleep," Vane ordered his pilot.

The sloop that Vane and his crew had stolen from Nassau was now full of cannon shot from the engagement with the heavy English frigate. She was on her last leg and if the gap in her hull ruptured anymore she, the crew, and her eight 12-pounders would be soon be sinking to the depths.

"Mr. England, she is a beauty and she looks to be a French frigate, probably hunting the likes of us," Vane said as Mr. England and Mr. Yeates approached the helm.

"Aye Captain, do we take the risk?" Mr. England asked.

"We have no choice, with our vessel doomed for the bottom and us needing more cannon to help retrieve our property, we must take her now," Vane said as he stepped aside to let Mr. Yeates take over the helm.

"Mr. England, it's going to take a bold move for an attack in the middle of the night. Except for the lookouts, the crew should be asleep and they will not have the time to start blasting away with cannon fire if we can surprise them," Vane said as he and Mr. England gathered the crew to reveal their plan.

"Men, our ship is about to go under and for us to live and get back what is rightly ours, we need this frigate," Vane shouted to the crew to instill fear and to encourage them to fight for their lives.

"We will have to take this ship brazenly and with no quarter for those who stand in our way," Vane sternly advised the crew and then put in motion the plan to take the frigate.

Regardless of the ships injury, Vane's sloop was still faster than the frigate. The night was moonless, the seas were only two to three feet, and the frigate was sailing with just the main and mizzen sails set.

"Mr. Yeates, you need to get our sloop as close to their stern as possible and keep her there so the men can hook her," Vane said earnestly as Mr. Yeates closed in on the stern of the frigate.

The lookouts on the frigate were either drunk, asleep, or both because no warming was given that night. The pyrates were able to sink two grappling hooks into the frigates stern, ascend the ropes, and then climb aboard. At the point of a dozen swords the pilot and the first mate dropped their weapons. The pyrates made their way to the cabins below and seized the Captain who surrendered only after a pistol was pointed to his head.

"Thank you Captain, a fine looking frigate with twenty-four cannons," Vane said to the French Captain as they stood on the deck of the stern and the sun's light broke on the horizon.

"French seamen, you have an opportunity to join us. You'll be free to choose your own destiny and no longer under the shackles of the French Navy. Who will join us?" Vane shouted from the deck of the frigates stern.

Only a few hands went up. They had been treated poorly and many had died of scurvy and punishment but to turn pyrate was immediate death if caught.

"Mr. England, find out who are the ship's doctor, carpenter, and cook and detain them with the volunteers. Transfer the Captain and his crew to the sloop and bring back the long boat," Vane ordered as he turned to go below to his new cabin.

In the Captain's cabin, Vane found an arsenal of pistols and rifles and the latest French maps of the Caribbean. Vane was studying the maps when Mr. England and Mr. Yeates entered the cabin.

"Captain, all is ready to set sail, in which direction do you think we can find our ship?" Mr. England asked as he admired a matching pair of new French pistols.

"Mr. Langford turned for the gold and silver and he knows these waters better than anyone. He would not head for Port Royal with such a treasure because that's where he thinks I would look first," Vane suspected as he studied the map.

"My guess is the Leeward Islands where they would seek a Governor who would look the other way for the right settlement," Vane assumed as he pointed to the islands on the map and then looked Mr. England straight in the eye.

"Mr. England, our direction is southeast, without delay and as swift as this ship can carry us," Vane ordered as he pounded the table.

"Captain, I'll be taking these pistols for the coming fight," Mr. England said as he placed them in his coat pockets.

"There are plenty. Mr. Yeates, take two pistols for yourself. Now, let's make this frigate fly," Vane ordered snarling as he pounded the table again, sending Mr. England and Mr. Yeates scrambling for the main deck.

Chapter 19

"Captain Bellamy, it has been days with no sign of another ship," Captain La Buse said as they stood on the deck of the stern.

"Aye, but we are headed in the right direction," Bellamy said confidently.

"As we drifted away from Vane's ship, several of the crew saw the ship turn and head eastward toward the islands of Catt and Long," Bellamy said as he placed two loaded pistols in his sash which La Buse had given to him earlier.

"With the storm coming from the southeast they would have sailed to the northeast to escape it and then the ship could have been blown even further off course by the storm," Bellamy presumed.

"Then where?" Captain La Buse asked.

"Mr. Langford and I were going to find a suitable island such as Catt Island to distribute the wealth amongst the crew," Bellamy said without divulging any information about the chests in Captain Vane's cabin.

"But Mr. Langford would probably have abandoned that plan since he had already discussed it with me and he would not go to either Nassau Harbor or Port Royal with such wealth. They would want to sail as far away from Vane as possible," Bellamy suspected.

"Could it be Hispaniola or the Leeward Islands?" La Buse asked while looking Bellamy straight in the eye.

"Yes and there are plenty of ships sailing near Hispaniola that can be seized on the way to the islands, if we have to go that far," Bellamy replied.

Hispaniola

Used as the rendezvous for Spanish treasure ships in the 16th Century, Hispaniola eventually became a major location for privateering and pyrating by the English, French and Dutch in the 17th and 18th Centuries.

The catastrophic destruction of the 1502 De Torres fleet of 32 ships (3,000,000 pesos), the 1553 Armada of Columbus of 16 ships (30,000,000 pesos), and the 1567 Terra Firma Armada (3,000,000 pesos) by hurricanes convinced the Spanish to move the rendezvous location to Havana and its protected harbor.

The English, French, and Dutch pyrates then found many hiding places along the mostly empty shores of Hispaniola from which they could prey on the ships sailing throughout the eastern Caribbean Sea. [1.4]

£

Mr. England and Mr. Yeates had rallied the crew and made the newly acquired French frigate sail as quickly as the wind was blowing. On the second night with a near waxing moon, a crewman caught sight of a ship in the distance.

"Captain, we have a ship heading southeast," Mr. Yeates shouted as he opened Captain Vane's cabin door.

"Yeates, what direction is it headed?" Vane asked waking from a drunken sleep. Vane was relying on rum to calm his infuriation at losing such a valuable cargo and his anxiety at trying to get it back.

"Southeast, as we are," Yeates shouted out as he turned and went back on deck.

The two ships were miles apart off the northern coast of Hispaniola, barely able to see each other except for the reflection of the moonlight from the white sails. Vane stumbled from his cabin onto the deck where England and Yeates were staring at what they hoped was their stolen ship.

"Blast it Mr. England, is it our ship?" Vane barked as he stumbled again, catching the railing to stop himself from going over the side.

"Captain, it looks to be the right ship but we will need to get closer to tell," England said continuing to gleam as much as possible with only the scant amount of light.

"Mr. England, have the crew lay on maximum sail now and at first light have them load all the cannons with only hammer shot, we want to stop her, not sink her," Vane ordered as he headed back to his cabin.

At first light Mr. Langford spotted a ship sailing faraway in the distance and to the west. He could not determine which way it was sailing so he only kept a close eye on it as they maintained a steady course for San Juan in the Leeward Islands.

"Mr. Langford, how is she sailing this morning?" Louis asked as he came up on deck.

"Good Captain, we have had full sail all night and we are just now approaching Hispaniola to the south," Mr. Langford said as he stepped aside to let Louis take the helm.

"There is a ship in the distance to the west and it appears to be heading southeast as we are. I kept our maneuvers to only what was needed and our distance has stayed the same," Mr. Langford said as he started to make his way below deck to wake the rest of the crew.

"Mr. Langford, have the crew to set maximum sail now. We can't take any chances on a ship of any sort coming up behind us," Louis shouted out to Mr. Langford.

"Aye Captain," Mr. Langford replied as he stepped down the stairs to the main deck.

Bellamy and La Buse spent hours in the captain's cabin speculating on where Langford must have taken Vane's Ship. Every time they came up with the same conclusion that Langford must be heading for the Leeward Islands.

"La Buse, I have changed my mind, I do not think we should look for another ship to acquire, it would take up valuable time that could be used in hunting down Vane's ship," Bellamy advised as they both explored possibilities on the French maps that La Buse had used during the war.

"I agree, by now we are almost north of Hispaniola" La Buse said as he reached for a bottle and poured more rum.

"Langford and the ship could be anywhere, but we are playing our best assumption and we will catch up to them soon," La Buse declared confidently just as they heard someone running down the stairs and then to their cabin.

"Captain, a ship, off the port bow," Mr. Noland shouted as he burst into the cabin and then turned and ran back up the stairs.

Both captains bounded for the door and up the ships stairs onto the main deck. On deck all eyes were searching for the ship that was far off in the distance, it appeared to come and go as the sunlight bounced off its white sails.

Captain La Buse ordered his crew to lay on as much sail as possible in hopes of chasing down the ship and told the gunners to load only double head shot for maximum carnage.

Chapter 20

"Captain, we are closing the gap but that ship is almost as quick as this frigate," Mr. England told Captain Vane as they stood on the deck of the stern and watched the ship in the distance.

"If it is our stolen ship then we have a task ahead of us in running her down," Vane replied as he looked through his scope at the ship.

"Mr. England, lighten our load," Vane ordered as he put his scope away and started for his cabin.

"Start with the supplies in the ship's hold but not the powder or shot. That's special for them who borrowed our ship," Vane said with a grin and started down the stairs to his cabin.

"Bellamy, they are throwing supplies overboard," La Buse shouted as he peered through his scope at the French frigate.

"There is another ship ahead of it in the distance," La Buse added as he joined Bellamy on the stern's deck and handed him the scope.

"We are chasing a French frigate who appears to be chasing another ship," Bellamy said as he lowered the scope.

"This French frigate is acting strangely. The French would not throw away good supplies just to chase down another ship unless it was full of silver," La Buse declared as he realized what he had just said.

"Could it be that the lead ship is Vane's ship?" Bellamy said as he looked through the scope more closely at the first ship.

"I hope it is and we will take her no matter what the cost," La Buse vowed.

"The French frigate is larger than ours but we are faster and it looks like we have about the same number of cannon," Bellamy speculated as he looked closer at the French frigate through the scope.

"La Buse, we need to make our way around the frigate, staying out of the range of her cannon, and make our way towards the lead ship?" Bellamy advised as he gave the scope back to La Buse.

La Buse agreed and gave the order.

"Captain Vane, there is a ship behind us," Mr. Yeates yelled out from the helm.

"Blast it, what curse is upon us that we should command so much torment, can it get any worse?" Vane barked from the starboard rail and started to make his way back to the helm.

"Mr. England what do you make of it?" Vane demanded as he approached the helm.

"Captain, it's a frigate like this one, only smaller with less cannon and no flag," England replied as he brought his scope down and stared at the advancing ship.

"What is she up too?" Vane thought out loud.

"She should be flying her flag as we are, unless she is a pyrate," Vane said as he started to consider his options.

"Mr. England, can you make out who is on board the frigate?" Vane asked clutching the rail.

England tried several times to focus his scope on the frigate but it was still too far away to determine who was on board the ship.

"Mr. England, if this frigate were honest it would be flying her flag and should have saluted by cannon," Vane concluded as he pointed out one of the crew near the main mast who was wearing a black shirt.

"You there, take down the French flag and fly your black shirt," Vane ordered the pyrate who ran to the stern and replaced the French flag with his black shirt.

"La Buse, it's the black flag, they are pyrates," Bellamy eagerly said as they stood by the railing.

"Curse the dog, it can't be Vane," La Buse silently implored.

"La Buse, do you see it?" Bellamy said troubled by La Buse's lack of enthusiasm.

"Yes, now we need to find out who they are," La Buse insisted as he ordered their black flag to be raised.

"La Buse, it's possible we could join forces if that lead ship is Vane's ship," Bellamy proposed as he thought about being able to get back the treasure he had lost.

"What if it's Vane on the French frigate?" La Buse questioned Bellamy who went from being exhilarated to mindful of whose valuable cargo it belonged to.

"If it's Vane on that ship he might use us but then he might kill us after we have served his purpose. Vane can't be trusted any further than you can throw a cannon ball," La Buse advised Bellamy as he paced back and forth between the helm and the railing, brooding over what to do.

"We can try to parlay and see if it works but we will have an escape plan just in case," La Buse told Bellamy as he summoned the crew to explain their strategy.

Captain Vane, having seen the frigate's black flag raised, ordered less sail so the frigate could get closer. As La Buse's frigate started to pull up close to the stern of Vane's French frigate the Captains could finally see one another.

"Blast it, it's La Buse, men fire your cannons now," Vane roared out the order to sink La Buse's ship.

"Drop both anchors and helmsman, hard to starboard, quickly," La Buse ordered his crew.

La Buse's frigate dug into the waves bringing it almost to a complete halt as it bobbed in the water like a cork. Only two cannon balls had caught the bow as Vane's frigate sailed on after the lead ship. La Buse saw Vane lift his finger in defiance as he ordered his crew to hoist the anchors.

"Mr. Nolan, sail for the lead ship but give us a wide berth between us and the French frigate," La Buse ordered Bellamy's quartermaster who had taken over at the helm.

"Why didn't you tell me you and Vane had a feud," Bellamy asked La Buse as they made their way to the bow.

"I wasn't sure if it was that big of a consequence for Vane," La Buse replied as he checked two of the pyrates who had taken wood splinters when the double headers hit the bow.

"And just what was the consequence," Bellamy asked as he checked the bow for any major cracks.

"Vane and his crew sailed into Port Royal with two sloops thieved near the Virgin Islands. We needed supplies to leave port so we helped ourselves to some of the stolen ship supplies while they went from bar to bar getting wasted on Jamaican rum," La Buse said amused at how easy the takings were.

"I guess word got back to Vane and he has taken offense at the deed and now holds a grudge," La Buse said as he observed how the mizzen fore and aft sail were slack in the wind.

"Mr Noland, track to leeward and keep the sails full," La Buse ordered as Mr. Noland adjusted the rudder to take advantage of the favorable wind.

Chapter 21

"Mr. Langford, there are now two ships behind us and one is quickly closing," Louis said as he stepped aside so Langford could take over the helm.

"Captain Louis, these ships look the size of frigates that have cannon," Langford said as he pointed to the top sail and one of the crew went aloft to adjust it.

"Worse case will be if Vane is on one ship and Bellamy is on the other ship," Louis replied as he placed his scope in his pocket.

Mr. Langford thought this as well. If it was true and Vane and Bellamy caught him, they would both torture him until he begged them to end his life quickly.

"Mr. Langford, what do you know of this coast?" Louis asked as he watched the two ships advance closer.

"In the distance, there is a harbor called Scots Bay, but it has only rocky ledges with no place for crew to go ashore," Mr. Langford apprised Louis as he glanced back over his shoulder to see how much ground the two ships had gained.

"Captain Louis, the ships are gaining on us, have you considered some sort of a plan to get us out of this quandary," Mr. Langford inquired respectfully.

"I can see them now through the scope, Vane is on the ship to starboard and Bellamy is on the ship to port. Both ships are flying the black flag," Louis said as he turned away from the railing and departed rapidly down to the Captain's cabin.

"Mr. England, it appears that our close friend Mr. Langford is at the helm of our ship," Captain Vane declared as he observed through his scope.

"Captain, La Buse has almost caught up to our ship, what's our plan," England said as they both stood near the helm of the French frigate.

"Let LaBuse sail past our ship," Vane said.

"Then, LaBuse will get to our ship first," England replied.

"That's what we want to happen. Let La Buse slug it out with Mr. Langford and after they are both wasted, we go in and take back what belongs to us," Vane said as he lowered his scope.

"Mr. Langford how far do you think we are from Scots Bay," Louis said as he emerged from the cabins below.

"Captain, it's only a few more miles," Mr. Langford said noticing the sack Louis was now carrying.

"Men, we're in for a scrap, we'll fire the starboard cannons first, get ready," Louis yelled out to the crew.

"Mr. Langford, I'll take the helm if you will take command of the cannon fire. And Mr. Langford, anything can happen, just do what I say, when I say it, and we all might get out alive," Louis said as he spun the wheel to starboard.

La Buse was taken by surprise. Vane's ship was turning about and now headed straight for his ship. La Buse ordered his crew to the cannons but they were all scattered throughout the ship, many still in the rigging adjusting the sails.

"Mr. Langford, fire when ready," Louis ordered.

As soon as the ship was just past the bow of LaBuse's ship, Mr. Langford's crew let fly the double head shot from fourteen cannon. The cannon shot sliced through La Buse's ship and crew like hot knifes through butter. The double head shot dismembered the bodies of many of La Buse's crew and tore through the mizzen mast, bringing it crashing down onto the deck.

La Buse's crew was able to fire several sporadic cannon shots that inflicted some but not near the damage that La Buse's ship and crew sustained. Louis turned Vane's ship about to bring his port side cannons to face La Buse's frigate. His crew worked quickly to reload the starboard cannons and then manned the port cannons in time to face off again with La Buse's ship.

This time La Buse was ready as both ships released their cannon shot on each other. It was devastating for the ships and their crew as rigging collapsed, sails toppled and crew members were killed or mutilated by the flying iron hammers. The main mast of Vane's ship was split in two and fell to the deck almost crushing the helm and Mr. Langford.

Louis sailed Vane's ship forward with only the mizzen mast providing sail to move the ship. Louis knew that there was only one thing left to do to save himself and the crew. La Buse still had his main mast that propelled his ship quickly towards Vane's ship.

"Captain Louis, Scots Bay," Mr. Langford pointed as he helped one of the injured crew to move away from the falling main mast.

Louis now saw that the bay was entombed by high rocky ledges with nowhere to place a ship and there was only one way of getting to shore.

"Mr. Langford, prepare to go ashore as soon as we stop, with no delay, understood?" Louis yelled as he pointed the ship to a ledge that was more accommodating than any other.

"Understood, Captain," Mr. Langford replied as he ordered the crew to get ready to throw grappling hooks on his command.

Louis maneuvered Vane's ship closer to dock with the rocky ledge. The ship scraped against the rocks which started tearing into the ships hull creating a loud ominous noise that evolved into sharp shrills as though the ship was crying out for mercy.

Mr. Langford ordered the crew to let fly the grappling hooks which found their target and held the ship close to the ledge. The crew secured the hooks and while the men scrambled to disembark, Louis tied down the helm, grabbed his sack, and ran for the rail.

The ship was mortally wounded and was starting to take on seawater as Louis jumped over the rail and onto the rocks. Looking back to seaward he saw La Buse's ship entering the harbor with La Buse and Bellamy standing at the rail with expressions of disbelief on their faces.

The two Captains couldn't believe that Louis had deliberately sailed Vane's ship onto the rocks, putting all of the gold and silver in jeopardy.

"LaBuse, the dog has sent our treasure to the bottom of the harbor," Bellamy yelled in agony over losing the valuable cargo.

"There's nothing we can do, Vane is right behind us to salvage what he can from the harbor floor," LaBuse resolved as he turned the ship in the direction of the Leeward Islands.

"Blast it, can nothing go our way," Vane shouted out from the helm as he watched his ship loaded with the Spanish gold and silver slip deeper into the waters of the harbor.

"Mr. England, it appears that we will need to go a wrecking once more," Vane said as he grasped the rails.

"Drop the anchor. Longboats over the side," Mr. England ordered as they all prepared to get back what was theirs.

Chapter 22

At the top of the cliff, Louis and his crew looked back down at Vane's ship as the waves rushed over its decks and started filling the hull with seawater. They could see LaBuse's ship sailing off towards the east and Captain Vane at the stern of his ship as it approached the sinking ship full of the Spanish gold and silver.

"Vane will not like having to dive for the silver but his crew should be able to pull most of it out of the wreck," Mr. Langford speculated as he helped one of the injured crewmen to stand and start to walk.

"We did it before and Captain Vane can do it again," Mr. Langford said as he headed for the jungle tree line beyond the cliff.

"Captain Louis, I noticed the sack that you've had even before you wrecked a perfectly good ship on the harbor rocks, will it be getting us out of this predicament?" Mr. Langford asked as they started walking down a jungle trail.

"If we can make it to the other side of this island then this sack will probably be our salvation," Louis said as he avoided a coiled snake lying at the foot of an old dead log.

As they moved into a clearing with a creek meandering through it, they stopped to make camp so they could attend to the two wounded crewmen and get a fire started. One of the men had taken a blow to the mid torso from double head shot and was coughing up blood. The other man had taken a large wooden splinter from the main mast to his right leg and it needed to be sewn up to stop the bleeding.

There wasn't much that they could do for the man hit by the double-head shot except give him some water from the creek and gather a pile of palm leaves so he could rest his head. He was in agony and still coughing up blood, most knew that he would probably be dead by the first morning light.

Mr. Langford attended to the other crewman who needed his leg sewn up. If they were on the ship, there would be sail needles available that were used to fix torn sails. Out in the jungle, with no needles, Mr. Langford improvised by taking palm leaves and tearing them into strips. Taking the strips one by one, he wrapped and tied each strip around the leg to pull the muscle and skin together so that it was as close as possible. Mr. Langford then took enough damp moss from a tree to cover the wound and placed it on top of the palm strips. He finished dressing the wound by picking several palm leaves, wrapping them around the leg to hold the moss in place, and tying it down with vine cordage. The field dressing wasn't pretty but it greatly increased the man's chances of survival and not losing his leg all together.

Two of the crew had started working on building a fire while the others gathered small trees, large palm leaves and vines for cordage to build several quick shelters. They didn't have time to build a suitable shelter which would keep them off the jungle floor, so they built several small shelters around and close to the fire.

Most of the crew knew that night time in the jungle was when predators like snakes, scorpions, and spiders go looking for something to eat. The few crewmen who had not experienced a night in the jungle were fixing to have a rude awakening.

Mr. Langford took the first watch and as Louis started to close his eyes he heard a cutting noise and saw Mr. Langford stabbing at the ground with his long knife. Mr. Langford stabbed a couple of more times and then stopped and raised the knife up to the campfire light to reveal a six inch black scorpion dangling on the point of his knife.

During the night, only a few of the men were able to sleep. The sleeping men's snoring, the injured crewman's agonizing moans, the relentless insect attacks, and the anxiety over the noises coming from just outside the camp kept most of the men on edge and sleepless.

As light finally made its way into the jungle clearing, the men found the crewman who was injured from the cannon shot close to the creek and dead. His agonizing pain must have caused him to crawl towards the water where he probably thought there might be some sort of relief.

Mr. Langford helped the crewman with the cut leg stand up and he grimaced from the excruciating pain that shot through his leg like a lightning bolt. He didn't want to be left behind so he took the pain and carried on, limping but alive and in good spirits.

They trekked through Jungle overgrowth for most of the morning until they reached a clearing where they could finally see the ocean in the distance.

"Mr. Langford, we made it," Louis shouted out as he stood on the top of an outcropping that overlooked the ocean. Looking down the coast, in the distance, he could see the bay and the town of Santo Domingo.

They continued traveling over the rugged terrain, attempting to make it to the town before nightfall but it was still too far in the distance. They were able to make it to the ocean, about ten miles from the town, where they set up camp and were able to find crabs and clams in abundance along the shore.

"Mr. Langford, now is the time to go into town and see what is available. I'll go alone, so as not to draw any attention. You stay with the men and I should be back before mornings light," Louis said as he grabbed his sack and set off down the shoreline towards town.

It was just after midnight when Louis reached the town where he went straight to the docks to see what might be available. There were two merchant ships and three sloops tied at the docks with all but one of the sloops looking seaworthy.

As Louis headed back towards the taverns he looked for a tree loaded with foliage and which had plenty of limbs for climbing. Finding one he checked to make sure no one was around and then he climbed to the top and tied his sack to a limb that was sturdy enough to hold it.

Back on the ground he proceeded to the street where most of the taverns were established. It was late at night and most of the customers were drunk or close to that point. Entering one that was still busy he asked the bartender who might own any of the sloops tied at the docks. The bartender motioned to a fellow in the corner with his back against the wall and said his name was Captain Marley.

"Good evening to you, sir. Might I have a word with you about your sloop?" Louis inquired respectively.

"Well lad, so you want to know about my ship, do you?" Captain Marley replied looking up from his mug of rum.

Louis could tell that he was an old seafaring Captain with probably many years of sailing experience on the high seas. His appearance was rough and unshaven with his large Captain's hat at a tilt and a pistol sash lying diagonally across his old dirty coat.

"Yes sir, I was wondering if she might be for sale?" Louis asked as he pulled up a chair.

"Well lad, for the right price, everything is for sale," Captain Marley said as he finished off his rum.

"Can we go take a look at her and let me inspect the decks below?" Louis said without hesitation.

"By the looks of you I doubt you have what it will take to make me part with my only ship," Captain Marley bluntly declared as he motioned for two rums.

Louis reached into his shirt pocket and pulled out a large ring. He shined it off on his shirt as a young lady placed two mugs of rum on the table and after she left with her silver he laid the ring on the table in front of Marley.

Marley almost had a heart attack as he gasped for air and then swooped the ring up with his right hand and placed it on the index finger of his left hand. It was a large gold ring with an emerald the size of a commodores coat button.

"This be a queens piece no less," Marley proclaimed as he admired the ring. "Where did you find such an exquisite jewel?"

"There are more where that came from and they are yours if the sloop is in good condition," Louis proposed as he finished off his rum.

"Lad, be this off of the Spanish wrecks I've been hearing so much of lately?" Marley snapped back as if suddenly aroused from a trance.

"It doesn't matter from where it came. Now, let's go take a look at your vessel if you want to make a trade?" Louis proposed as he pushed his chair back and stood up.

Captain Marley led the way to the docks, telling Louis all the way what a fine ship it was. Just before reaching the docks, Louis told Marley to go ahead and that he would be there shortly. Louis retrieved his sack from the tree and then rejoined Marley at his sloop. After boarding and looking throughout the ship they entered the Captain's cabin where Captain Marley poured more rum and they both sat down at the table.

"Now Lad, about your suggestion, I had not been thinking about parting with a sloop of this quality. She is well built, solid, and fast for any getaway," Captain Marley said as he eyed the sack Louis had put down at the foot of his chair.

"Captain, what's your price? I have urgent matters elsewhere. Let's get on with this," Louis said growing impatient with the old man's dickering tactics.

"Well lad, since you want to get this over quickly, I'll be taking everything that you have in that sack of yours," Marley said pointing to the sack.

At that moment, Louis felt the cold hard steel of a pistol pressed against the back of his ear.

"Mr. Ansel, tie the lad up and we'll drop him off on the way to Port Royal," Marley ordered as he pushed his chair back and stood up.

At that moment, Mr. Langford entered the room with pistols cocked in both hands, pointing one at Ansel and the other one at Marley.

"Mr. Ansel, slowly put the pistol on the table and lie down on the floor. Marley you do the same," Mr. Langford ordered.

"Langford, join us and we will split the sack three ways," Marley suggested as he dropped to his knees and then laid down on the floor next to Mr. Ansel.

"Not this time Marley. Captain Louis would you get us some rope," Mr. Langford said as he kept the pistols pointed at the two pyrates.

"Langford, it's good to see you again. I wish it were under more agreeable circumstances," Marley said lifting his head off the floor and looking up towards Mr. Langford.

"Marley I figured you would be dead by now, either hung from the gallows or of old age," Mr. Langford said as he moved back to let Louis tie the hands of Marley and Ansel.

"They haven't caught me yet and they never will. I'll go out fighting and no less," Marley said as he snarled and struggled with the rope that now tied his hands together.

"Captain Louis, do we sail this sloop back to our camp where we can pick up the crew and finish this business?" Mr. Langford asked as Louis finished tying the hands of Mr. Ansel.

"Yes, Mr. Langford and well done. I'll get the ships ropes clear from the dock and you can start preparing the main sail for hoisting," Louis told Mr. Langford as he left the cabin and started up the stairs to the main deck.

Louis lifted off the bow and stern ropes, then pulled each rope onto the ship as it slowly moved away from the dock. Joining Mr. Langford, they both started to hoist the main sail that immediately caught the wind and began to move the ship forward. Louis ran to the helm and turned the wheel to port as the ship slowly moved out to sea in the darkness.

"Mr. Langford, I'm glad you decided to follow me," Louis said as he lined the ship up parallel to the shore and headed towards the camp.

"I knew what you were trying to accomplish, I just wanted to make sure you could do it," Mr. Langford replied as he watched for the light from their campfire.

The men at the camp awoke to a sloop lying just offshore and four men in a launch coming ashore.

"Men, we have our ship with thanks to Captain Marley and Mr. Ansel," Mr. Langford shouted out as Louis untied their hands.

"Now Captain Marley, here is the emerald ring that you were mesmerized with plus four other rings that should more than adequately pay for your sloop and if you follow the shoreline to the south, it will get you back to town," Louis said as he pointed in the direction of town.

"My ship is worth more than five rings, you flea bitten dog. You better hope our paths do not cross again and if they do, I'll cut you into little pieces," Marley shouted out as he and Ansel started running down the shoreline.

"You old mangy dog, you better be glad we didn't hang you from the closest tree and then feed your carcass to the buzzards," Louis shouted out after Marley, laughing with the men as Marley and Ansel started running as fast as they could.

"Okay men, to the ship," Louis ordered.

"A ship, finally a ship," Carmen yelled out to the others from the beach.

Juan was the first to reach the beach followed by Carlos and Maria. They had lost count of the days since Louis and Mr. Langford had left them stranded on the island and now they were jubilant at the site of salvation.

They immediately set the two signal fires, piling on green palm leaves for maximum smoke.

"They see the smoke. Their turning towards us," Carlos yelled as they all waved, jumping up and down, happy that someone at last had come. When the ship got close to shore, the crew dropped anchor and lowered a launch over the side.

The joyfulness didn't last for long.

"Wipe that grin off your face. You lying, brainless, worm headed, sack of dead fish," Carmen screamed at Louis as he jumped from the longboat.

"What were you thinking when you left us on this God forsaken hell hole. You disgusting, ignorant, filthy, low life," Carmen yelled as she continued to scream into Louis's face.

"Do you know what it is like to be left on an island without any hope of a ship coming by this rat hole? This island is out in the middle of nowhere, no ships have come by since you left, what did you expect us to do?" Carmen shouted as she through her arms into the air and looked Louis in the face for some kind of a logical answer.

"Please senorita, calm down," Louis begged.

"We did it to keep you out of harm's way. Vane would have eventually come by to check this island, he would have seen the ship and we would all be dead," Louis said as he opened his arms for forgiveness but Carmen did not forgive.

"Come, we have something to show you," Louis said climbing back into the launch and offering his hand to Carmen.

"This better be good or you will never hear the end of it," Carmen said as she took his hand and climbed into the launch.

Once everyone was aboard the sloop they weighed anchor and sailed into the cove where the raft was still anchored.

"Look down to the bottom," Louis told them as they all stood at the sloops starboard railing.

They all clutched the railing and peered over the side and looked at the bottom through the clear water where chests of gold and silver were scattered over the ocean floor.

"We left you the four chests of silver and dropped most of the other chests here before sailing off. We kept two of the chests filled with gold in the Captain's cabin and many chests of the silver down below. We imagine that Vane scared off La Buse and recovered what we left on his sinking ship. Hopefully that will cure his appetite and he'll leave us alone," Louis said as he stepped back and put his hand on the wheel.

"So where do we go from here," Louis asked

"Back to Cartagena," they all chimed in together.

"Mr. Langford, can you get us to Cartagena," Louis asked

"Aye Captain, as quick as the wind can carry us," Mr. Langford said as he and the crew started preparations to bring the gold and silver aboard.

£

Epilogue

Captain Charles Johnson in his 1724 London publication, *A General History of the Robberies and Murders of the Most Notorious Pyrates*, gave reasons and causes for the current discontent of seaman. Captain Johnson explained: *"that there are Multitudes of Seaman at this day unemploy'd; it is too evident by their straggling, and begging all over the kingdom. Nor is it so much their Inclination to Idleness, as their own hard Fate, in being cast off after their work is done, to starve or steal. I have not known a Man of War commission'd for several Years past, but three times her Compliment of Men have offer'd themselves in 24 Hours; the Merchants take their Advantage of this, lessen their Wages, and those few [Seaman] who are in Business are poorly paid, and but poorly fed; such Usage breeds Discontents among them; and makes them eager for any Change."* [10]

Manuel Schonhorn, in postscript (1999), explained that *"by 1715 the English Navy had discharged about three-quarters of its men; of almost 54,000 who had been on the books when the war began, by 1717 less than 12 percent retained employment."* Schonhorn further explained that *"Privateering crews, once military adjuncts to the naval forces recruited to disrupt enemy trade, were now no longer licensed by the warring powers."* [20]

Captain Johnson saw only two ways to remedy the evil of pyracy: *"either to find Employment for the great Numbers of Seaman turn'd adrift at the conclusion of a war, and thereby prevent their running into such Undertakings, or to guard sufficiently the Coast of Africa, the West-Indies, and other Places where to Pyrates resort."* [10]

Captain Benjamin Hornigold

Captain Benjamin Hornigold was sporadically discussed by Captain Johnson in his 1724 London publication but it was only later that the full extent of Hornigold's endeavors were recognized. Hornigold was indeed the mentor for Sam Bellamy (Black Sam), Paulsgrave Williams, Edward Teach (Blackbeard), Oliver La Buse (the Buzzard) and other pyrates during his six year stint (1713-1719) as a pyrate Captain and Commodore. Out of the bowels of Port Royal came Hornigold and his pyrate gang who sailed to Nassau and started their enterprise in 1713 with only three canoes. Hornigold built up his pyrate operation through bold aggressive maneuvers that won him valuable prizes and the following of hundreds of pyrates. In 1715 he was robbing the Spanish treasure wrecks on the Florida coast and by 1716 he and Edward Teach were sailing the *Adventure*, Sam Bellamy and Paulsgrave Williams were sailing the *Marianne*, and Oliver La Buse was sailing the *Postillion.* There were 200 pyrates aboard the three ships at their Hispanolia hideout and Commodore Hornigold was now in command of it all.

It all came crashing down in the summer of 1716 when the pyrates disagreed about whether or not to attack English vessels. Hornigold, born in Norfolk, England, always was reluctant to take English prizes. So, Hornigold, Teach and several loyal pyrates sailed the *Adventure* back to the Bahamas where their success continued and by 1717 they had captured many prize vessels with valuable cargos.

However, by the end of 1717, Hornigold had decided to take the pardon for pyrates offered by King George I and Teach became Blackbeard. Not only did Hornigold accept the pardon he joined Governor Woodes Rogers in hunting down the pirates who did not accept the pardon, like Captains Edward Teach, Paulsgrave Williams, Charles Vane, Edward England and Oliver La Buse, some of whom he had mentored and helped to get started in the business. Hornigold died in the pursuit of his associates and Captain Johnson writes in 1724 that *"Captain Hornigold, another of the famous Pyrates, was cast away upon Rocks, a great Way from Land, and perished."*

[10,11,12,13,14,15,16]

Captain Samuel Bellamy

Captain Samuel (Black Sam) Bellamy was born in England in 1689 and had a brief but successful stint as a pyrate. Captain Charles Johnson put Bellamy and Paulsgrave Williams at the Spanish Armada wrecks in 1715: *"Captain Bellamy and Paul Williams, in two sloops, had been upon a Spanish wreck, and not finding their Expectation answered, as has been mentioned in former Parts of this History, they resolved not to lose their Labour, and agreed to go upon the Account, a Term among the pyrates, which speaks their profession."* Around March of 1716, Bellamy and Williams allied themselves with Captain Benjamin Hornigold who entrusted Bellamy as the Captain of the *Marianne*. Another alliance came shortly thereafter when Captain Oliver La Buse joined Captain Hornigold with his armed sloop *Postillion* and the three captains created havoc among the commercial fleets by taking down merchant ships as quickly as they were spotted between the Bahamas Channel and the Leeward Islands.

A dispute with Hornigold in June, 1716 over his aversion to capturing English vessels saw Hornigold and Teach going back to Nassau and Bellamy, Williams, and La Buse continuing to rain mayhem on the English, French and Dutch commercial vessels in the Leeward Islands. La Buse and his pyrates later agreeably parted ways with Bellamy, seeking to strike out on their own. Bellamy and Williams thereafter took down a merchant ship (*Sultana*) that they converted into a square rigged pyrate ship with twenty-four cannon and along with the *Marianne* they were able to take down a prize that put Bellamy on the map.

The *Whydah* was a fast, 300 ton, eighteen cannon, English slave ship that had just sold its cargo and was loaded with gold and other valuable goods. She was making her way back home to England through the Bahamas when Bellamy and Williams captured her without a fight. They added ten more cannons to the *Whydah* and headed north (Bellamy now Commodore on the *Whydah* and Williams as Captain on the *Marianne*) taking down more merchant ships along the way and adding more ships to their fleet. However, life was usually short for a pyrate and when they were caught in a storm in April, 1717 near Cape Cod with 70 mile per hour winds and 30 foot seas, the Whydah sank with all 146 pyrates on board the ship including Commodore Bellamy.

[10,11,13,14,16]

Captain Paulsgrave Willams

Captain Paulsgrave Williams took care of the financing when he and Captain Bellamy started their partnership upon the

1715 Spanish Armada wrecks in Florida. The partnership lasted about eighteen months seeing Bellamy rise to the rank of Commodore and Williams to the rank of Captain among their pyrate comrades. When the *Whydah* sank in 1717, taking Bellamy with it, Williams sailed the *Marianne* back to Nassau to decide on their next course of action. Consorting with Edward Teach and Charles Vane, Williams was faced with either taking the pardon offered by the King, as Hornigold did in 1718, or leaving Nassau. Like many of the pyrates having to make that choice, Williams chose Africa and Madagascar, soon to be followed by fellow captains Oliver La Buse and Edward England.

[10,11,14,16]

Captain Oliver La Vasseur (La Buse)

Captain Oliver La Buse had a long run of good fortune that enabled him to lead a pyrates life from 1713 to 1730. It was an extremely long time since most pyrates did well if they could pyrate for two to three years and then make it out alive to spend their take. Good luck was especially with La Buse when he and his pyrate crew decided to split from Bellamy and Williams and go their separate ways. If they had followed Bellamy and the *Whydah*, they could have been seven fathoms deep and swimming with the fish.

La Buse and his pyrates chose not to except the Kings pardon and continued their pyrating ways in the islands until June, 1718. At that time, Colin Woodard puts La Buse in the Leeward Islands at La Blanquilla where he is cornered by Captain Francis Hume and the HMS *Scarborough*. La Buse is lucky again while trying to plunder a small prize sloop, he escapes in a faster sloop with most of his pyrate crew who decide that West Africa may prove to be a more profitable venture, if not safer.

La Buse eventually meets up with Captains Paulsgrave Williams, Howell Davis, and Thomas Cocklyn on the west coast of Africa, spending most of 1719 taking down slave ships. Later they attacked a Royal African Company fort at Sierra Leone and took everything of value. However, doing the celebration they had a falling out over old grievances from their past experiences in the Bahamas and parted company. Angus Konstam gives Captain Davis's parting words: *"Hark ye, Cocklyn and La Buse, I find by strengthening you, I have put a rod in your hands to whip myself, but I'm still able to deal with both of you; but since we met in love, let us part in love, for I find that three of a trade can never agree."*

Davis moved south capturing two English ships and a Dutch ship with thirty cannons. Davis and his pyrate crew then set sail for the Portuguese Island of Principe where the Governor was tricked about their identity and in retaliation he set an ambush that ended in the death of Davis. The crew took revenge by sacking and burning the town and the fort to the ground. The crew needed another captain and chose Bartholomew Roberts (Black Bart) who did not disappoint. Colin Woodard writes that "Roberts presided over what was probably one of the most productive pirate companies in history, taking over 400 vessels before they were captured by the Royal Navy in February 1722." Roberts engaged the HMS *Swallow* of fifty cannons at Whydah, West Africa, with his forty cannon *Royal Fortune*. Roberts was killed by the *Swallow's* first volley of grape-shot to the throat and his crew threw him overboard as he had told them to do. Fifty-four of his crew were captured, tried at Cape Coast Castle, found guilty of pyracy, and hanged in mass.

La Buse, lucky again not to have ended up on the Slave Coast with Roberts, sailed to Madagascar and met with John Taylor on St. Mary's's Island. Taylor, like La Buse, was a renegade from Nassau and he gave the veteran captain command of a fast sloop named the *Victory*. Angus Konstam writes what happens next: *"The two pirates sailed to La Reunion, where they came across the Nossa Senhora de Cabo, a homeward bound Portuguese merchantmen transporting the Count of Ericeira. The Portuguese ship had been dismasted in a storm, and proved to be easy pickings, being captured after a brief boarding action. The ship was laden with plunder, most notably a hoard of diamonds that the count planned to present to King Joao V of Portugal."*

A once in a lifetime opportunity, the valuables were divided up amongst the pyrates who then split up and went their separate ways. La Buse is said to have secretly established a home on the Seychelles archipelago where he hid his treasure stolen from the Portuguese galleon. La Buse's luck finally ran out when he was captured and taken to Saint-Denis, Reunion where he was hanged for pyracy in 1730.

[10,11,14,16]

Captain Henry Jennings

Captain Henry Jennings was a veteran seafaring captain with wartime experience and a country estate when the Governor of Jamaica offered him the command of the privateer warship *Barsheba*. When the 1715 Spanish Armada wrecked on the east coast of Florida, Jennings hired on extra crew including Charles Vane, Jack Rackham, and Edward England, stocked the *Barsheba* with more than enough supplies, and headed for the wrecks. Jennings found the main Spanish camp at the wreck of Ubilla's Capitana and stole 120,000 pesos in silver from Admiral Salmon. The Governor of Jamaica considered this pyracy but did not arrest Jennings who went back a second and third time for more of the Spanish silver. Each time they robbed the Spanish camp they sailed to a primitive encampment called Nassau in the Bahamas Islands to divide up the valuables. While Jennings was away from Jamaica the Governor was disposed and Jennings was now declared a pyrate.

Nassau was becoming a hub for pyrate activity and it was only a matter of time that the paths of Henry Jennings and Benjamin Hornigold would cross again. Colin Woodard explains that "There may have been bad blood from their privateering days in Jamaica or Jennings, an educated ship captain with a comfortable estate, may have looked down on Hornigold, who was likely a penniless sailor." Jennings had become the archenemy of Benjamin Hornigold and was mentor to Charles Vane, Jack Rackham, and Edward England. Hornigold, Teach, Bellamy and Williams would use persuasion and their wits to keep engagements less violent while Jennings, Vane, Rackham, and England were murderous villains who inflicted pain and agony much more readily than their counterparts.

Angus Konstam writes of the activity at Nassau: *"By the summer of 1717 over 500 pirates were reportedly using the island as a base, serving in at least a dozen small vessels – mainly sloops and brigantines. Men such as Benjamin Hornigold, Charles Vane, Henry Jennings, Edward England, Edward Teach (Blackbeard), and Sam Bellamy all passed through New*

Providence and called the island home during these heady years." Shortly thereafter King George I signed *A Proclamation for Suppressing Pyrates,* bringing the party to an end and offering a full pardon for pyracy and crimes thereof before January, 1718. If the pyrates did not accept the pardon they would be hunted down and in the majority of cases, hanged for their crimes. Benjamin Hornigold not only accepted the pardon but also turned on his comrades, became a pyrate bounty hunter, and died in their pursuit. Henry Jennings also accepted the pardon but he chose to retire to Bermuda where he lived another twenty-seven years on the wealth he accumulated as a pyrate.

[10,11,13,14]

Captain Charles Vane

Captain Charles Vane did not except the pardon offered by King George I in 1718 as eagerly as Jennings and Hornigold did. Vane was crude, mean, and sadistic, often treating his crew as badly as he treated the merchants that he plundered. Being double crossed by your brethren only helped fuel the fire for violent acts being perpetrated during engagements. Jennings had stolen several prizes from Hornigold at Nassau and Hornigold was overjoyed with Bellamy and Williams who stole valuable goods and 28,500 pesos in silver from Jennings and Vane. Vane then vented his vengeance by taking it out on merchant captains and their crews.

Over time, Vane developed just as many enemies from the pyrate brotherhood as he had from the King and the merchants who he plundered without mercy. When Captain

Pearse, commander of the *HMS Phoenix,* arrived in February, 1718 at Nassau to declare the proclamation of the King's pardon, pro-pardon pyrates told Pearse where they could find Vane. Pearse found the hideout and unleashed the *Phoenix's* cannons on Vane's sloop. Vane threw up the white flag and Pearse took them back to Nassau. David Cordingly wrote that some of the pro-pardon pyrates feared that Pearse would execute Vane and his crew so they told Pearse that more pyrates would sign the pardon if he released them. Pearse released them and he got the promised signatures.

The signatures meant a second chance to men like Hornigold and Jennings but it meant nothing to Vane, Rackham, and England. They were hardened criminals bent on self-destruction and anyone else that they could drag down with them. Angus Konstam writes of Vane's capture of two Bermudan sloops and from the owner's deposition saying *"Vane had beaten him and his men, and then tortured one of the crew by tying him up, then jabbing burning matches into his eyes. On the other sloop, Vane hanged one of the crew until he was almost dead, then slashed at him with his cutlass until his fellow pirates calmed him down. Clearly Charles Vane was something of a murderous psychopath, who was quickly gaining a reputation for cruelty."* Vane, Rackham, and England were now at war with the King's Navy, the pyrate bounty hunters like Hornigold, and their own kind who would turn them in for the reward money.

As it turned out it was not any of the above that brought an end to Vane's career, it was his own pyrate crew that was his demise. Captain Charles Johnson describes when Vane and his crew were chasing after a ship in 1718 and were surprised when *"she discharged a Broadside upon the Pyrate, and hoisted Colours, which shewed her to be a French Man of War. Vane desired to have nothing further to say to her, but trimm'd his Sails, and stood away from the French Man; but Monsieur having a Mind to be better informed who he was, set all his Sails, and crowded after him. During this chase, the Pyrates were divided in their Resolutions what to do; Vane the Captain, was for making off as fast as he could, alledging the Man of War was too strong to cope with; but one Jack Rackam, who was an Officer, that had a kind of a Check upon the Captain, rose up in Defense of a contrary Opinion, saying, that tho' she had more guns, and a greater Weight of Mettal, they might board her, and then the best Boys would carry the Day. Rackam was well seconded and the Majority was for boarding; but Vane urged, that it was too rash and desperate an Enterprise, the Man of War appearing to be twice their Force."* Vane, as captain, had the absolute power over the ship and told the crew to break off the engagement. Most of the crew were discouraged by Vane's actions and the next day they called for the test of a vote that ousted Vane and placed Rackham as the new captain of the *Ranger*.

Vane and the pyrates that supported him were given a sloop that was accompanying the *Ranger* and they set sail for the Gulf of Honduras. Vane and his crew quickly started capturing small vessels, trying to move up to a larger ship so that they could get back into the game. They were operating off of an island that Captain Charles Johnson called "Barnacko" when the sloop that Vane was sailing was thrown onto a small uninhabited island by a violent storm. The sloop was destroyed and most of Vane's crew had drowned in the storm.

Vane and what was left of his crew were castaways for several weeks upon the island until a ship looking for water arrived and took them aboard. Vane was later recognized by another visiting Captain onboard the ship and he was arrested and taken to Port Royal, Jamaica. There he stood trial, was convicted of pyracy, and then hanged at Gallows Point over looking Port Royal harbor in March, 1721. Thereafter his body was placed in a cage and hung at the entrance to the harbor. It was told that Vane called no witnesses and asked no questions at his trial and he did not express any remorse for his crimes before he swung from the gallows.

[10,11,12,13.14]

Captain Edward England

Captain Edward England, like Charles Vane, started privateering out of Port Royal, Jamaica and turned pyrate with his brethren on the 1715 Spanish Armada shipwrecks. The wealth that was strewn up and down the coast of Florida by the shipwrecks was just too much for the privateers to turn their backs on. So, they stole the gold and the silver from the Spanish, mostly by force at the point of a pistol. Captain Charles Johnson wrote that *"England, was one of these Men, who seemed to have a Share of Reason, as should have taught him better Things. He had a great deal of good Nature, and did not want for Courage; he was not avaritious, and always adverse to the ill Usage Prisoners received; He would have been contended with moderate Plunder, and less mischievous Pranks, could his Companions have been brought to the same Temper, but he was generally overruled, and as he was engaged in that abominable Society, he was obliged to be a partner in all their vile Actions."* [10]

England soon became Vane's first quartermaster and chose not to take the King's pardon along with Vane and Rackham when Commander Pearse and the *HMS Phoenix* sailed into Nassau with the King's proclamation. Whereas Vane and Rackham chose to stay and fight the incoming tide moving against pyracy, England chose to leave Nassau and seek his fortune off the waters of Africa and Madagascar. Operating off the coast of West Africa, England and his crew were doing well taking down nine merchant and slave ships in the spring of 1719. England was captain of the *Pearl* and he gave John Taylor, his quartermaster, command of another prize named the *Victory*.

After sailing to the Indian Ocean and establishing a base at Saint Mary's Island, England took another prize which was a thirty-four cannon three-masted ship that he made his flagship and named the *Fancy*. Unfortunately, they soon ran into two English East Indiamen ships carrying commissions to take pyrates. The ships engaged with little wind meaning that they could barely maneuver so they blazed away at each other with their cannons. Angus Konstam wrote that *"the fight lasted for three hours, and both sides fired broadsides into the other at close range until both vessels were holed and damaged."* England and Taylor defeated the English ships and England decided to show mercy and let them sail away even after some ninety pyrates had been killed in the battle.

Captain Taylor and what was left of the pyrate crew were angry about the mercy shown the English and later called for a vote which deposed England who was then marooned with three other pyrates on the island of Mauritius. Captain Charles Johnson wrote that *"Captain England and his companions having made a little Boat of Starves and old Pieces of Deal left there, went over to Madagascar; where they subsist at present on the Charity of some of their Brethren, who had made better Provision for themselves, than they had done."* England died shortly thereafter of disease but it is not clear whether he died a beggar or a wealthy man from the plunder he had buried on Saint Mary's Island.

[10,11,12,13.14]

£

Selected Bibliography

Burgess, Robert F. and Carl J. Clausen. *Florida's Golden Galleons: The Search for the 1715 Spanish Treasure Fleet.* Port Salerno: Florida Classics Library, 1982. [9]

Cordingly, David. *Under the Black Flag.* New York: Random House, 1995. [12]

Cordingly, David. *Pirate Hunter of the Caribbean.* New York: Random House, 2011. [13]

Hildred, Alexandra. *Weapons of Warre*: The Armaments of the Mary Rose. Portsmouth, England: The Mary Rose trust Ltd, 2011. [19]

Johnson, Captain Charles. *A General History of the Robberies and Murders of the Most Notorious Pyrates .* London, 1724 (reprinted by Routledge and Paul, London, 1955). [10]

Konstam, Angus. *Piracy: The Complete History.* Oxford: Osprey Publishing, 2008. [14]

Lavery, Brian. *The Arming and Fitting of English Ships of War 1600-1815.* London: Naval Institute Press, 1987. [17]

Little, Benerson. *How History's Greatest Pirates Pillaged, Plundered, And Got Away With It.* MA: Fair Winds, 2011. [15]

Marx, Robert F. *Spanish Treasure in Florida Waters.* Boston: Mariners Press, 1979. [2]

Marx, Robert F. *New World Shipwrecks: 1492-1825.* Dallas: Ram Publishing, 1994. [3]

Marx, Robert F. and J. Marx. *The Search for Sunken Treasure.* Toronto: Key Porter Books, 1993. [18]

Pringle, Patrick. *Jolly Roger: The Story of the Great Age of Piracy.* New York: Dover Publications, 2001. [16]

Potter, John S., Jr., *The Treasure Divers Guide, Revised Edition.* Garden City: Doubleday, 1972. [1]

Schonhorn, Manuel. *Daniel Defoe: A General History of the Pyrates* . New York, Dover Publications, 1999 [20]

Singer, Steven D. *Shipwrecks of Florida, Second Edition.* Sarasota: Pineapple Press, 1998. [6]

Wagner, Kip. *Pieces of Eight: Recovering the Riches of A lost Spanish Treasure Fleet.* New York: E.P. Dutton & Co, 1966. [8]

Walton, Timothy R. *The Spanish Treasure Fleets.* Sarasota: Pineapple Press, 1994. [4]

Weller, Robert. *Galleon Hunt.* West Palm Beach: Florida Treasure Brokers, 1992. [5]

Weller, Robert. *Sunken Treasure on Florida Reefs.* Lake Worth: Crossed Anchors Salvage, 1987. [7]

Woodard, Colin. *The Republic of Pirates.* New York: Harcourt Publishing, 2007. [11]

www.ingramcontent.com/pod-product-compliance
Lightning Source LLC
Chambersburg PA
CBHW030502260626
47157CB00005B/1615